THE SHORT FICTION OF FLANN O'BRIEN

Other Works by Flann O'Brien

NOVELS

The Poor Mouth

At Swim-Two-Birds

The Third Policeman

The Hard Life

The Dalkey Archive

COLLECTIONS

The Best of Myles

Further Cuttings from Cruiskeen Lawn

At War

Flann O'Brien: Plays and Teleplays

THE SHORT FICTION OF FLANN O'BRIEN

Edited by Neil Murphy and Keith Hopper, with
translations from the Irish by Jack Fennell

DALKEY ARCHIVE PRESS
CHAMPAIGN / LONDON / DUBLIN

"Naval Control" was originally published in *Amazing Stories Quarterly* in 1932, attributed to John Shamus O'Donnell, and is believed to be in the public domain. For more information see pp. xv and 146–149.

First edition, 2013

Library of Congress Cataloging-in-Publication Data

O'Brien, Flann, 1911–1966.
[Short stories. Selections]
The Short Fiction of Flann O'Brien / edited by Neil Murphy and Keith Hopper, with translations from the Irish by Jack Fennell. -- First edition.
pages cm
ISBN 978-1-56478-889-4 (pbk. : acid-free paper)
I. Murphy, Neil, editor of compilation. II. Hopper, Keith, editor of compilation. III. Title.
PR6029.N56A6 2013b
823'.912--dc23
2013012011

Partially funded by a grant from the Illinois Arts Council, a state agency.

www.dalkeyarchive.com

Cover: design and composition by Mikhail Iliatov, image by Eddie O'Kane

Printed on permanent/durable acid-free paper

Contents

Introduction: The Invisible Author

> Strictly speaking, this story should not be written or told at all. To write it or to tell it is to spoil it. This is because the man who had the strange experience we are going to talk about never mentioned it to anybody, and the fact that he kept his secret and sealed it up completely in his memory is the whole point of the story. Thus we must admit that handicap at the beginning—that it is absurd for us to tell the story, absurd for anybody to listen to it and unthinkable that anybody should believe it.
>
> —Flann O'Brien, "John Duffy's Brother," 1940

Throughout his career, the concept of the invisible author remained at the heart of Brian O'Nolan's (post-)modernist aesthetic—or as Myles na Gopaleen magisterially declared in 1964: "Compartmentation of personality for the purpose of literary utterance ensures that the fundamental individual will not be credited with a certain way of thinking and fixed attitudes. No author should write under his own name nor under one permanent pen name." For scholars, though, this principle of pseudonymity has become something of a bibliographical minefield: O'Nolan claimed to have written under a whole host of pen names, not all of which have been discovered or confirmed. This present collection includes work from several of these known pseudonyms, and proposes consideration of at least one new one. In Irish (Gaelic), our shadowy author writes under Brian Ó Nualláin, while in English he splits into many personas, including Brother Barnabas, Flann O'Brien, Myles na gCopaleen, Myles na Gopaleen, Lir O'Connor, and, eventually, Brian Nolan and Brian O'Nolan. In an appendix to this volume, we have also included a story by John Shamus O'Donnell, another possible *nom de plume*; this is accompanied by an invitation to Flanneurs to further investigate its likely authenticity as a work attributable to Flann O'Brien.

For the purposes of consistency we retain the name "Flann O'Brien" for general comment, although the original pen names remain at the head of each individual entry. Because our selections are drawn from several periods and sources (newspapers, magazines, journals, anthologies, and archives), they speak to a range of the larger works and yet simultaneously ask to be considered in their own terms, thereby opening up new alleyways and backstreets of discovery for O'Brien aficionados. Far from fragmenting the voice of "Flann O'Brien," the sheer multiplicity of pseudonyms—and the many posthumous, nameless, and playfully satirical narrators—ultimately act as a cohesive but dissonant statement that implicitly refutes the idea of a singular and authoritative centre of meaning. For O'Brien as much as Roland Barthes, the death of the author is the birth of the reader.

This anthology includes new translations of five Irish-language stories originally published in the early 1930s, prefaced with a brief introduction by the translator, Jack Fennell. These stories, while valuable in their own right, have interesting parallels with the early stories in English, and with the major novels which followed a few years later. "The Tale of Black Peter" ("Aistear Peadar Dubh"), and "Revenge on the English in the Year 2032!" ("Díoghaltais ar Ghallaibh 'sa Bhliain 2032!"), for instance, resonate strongly with the satire of Irish cultural politics that we later find in *An Béal Bocht* (first published in 1941; translated as *The Poor Mouth* in 1973). Similarly, "The Arrival and Departure of John Bull" ("Teacht agus Imtheacht Sheáin Bhuidhe") includes a scathingly parodic treatment of Irish myth and legend, which gives advance notice of Flann O'Brien's novelistic fascination with textuality and temporal play.

The same fascination with self-reflexive framing is evident in the English-language story "Scenes in a Novel," although the subject-matter is less obviously fixated on Irish culture. This early story from 1934 shows the nascent stirrings of some of the artistic processes that O'Brien would later explore in *At Swim-Two-Birds* (1939), including the principle of "aestho-autogamy" and the character revolt against the despotic author. "Scenes in a Novel" also features the mischievous use of mock footnotes—"indeed, the whole incident reminded me forcibly of Carruthers McDaid"*—and it inaugurates that most unreliable of narrative voices, the mordant storyteller who is "probably posthumous." Both of these elements, of course, prefigure the darkly comic machinations of *The Third Policeman* (completed in

*Who is Carruthers McDaid, you ask?

1940; first published in 1967), which is increasingly regarded as O'Brien's masterpiece.

Thus, several years in advance of his most important novels, many of O'Brien's metafictional ideas had already emerged in embryonic form. This deconstructive playfulness is still evident in the early 1940s: "When I Met William of Orange" (1942) presents itself as a "Footnote to the Battle of the Boyne," while "I'm Telling You No Lie!" (1943) purports to offer "Some leaves from the author's salad days." (Both of these stories, first published in the *Irish Digest*, are reprinted here for the first time.) In addition, stories such as "John Duffy's Brother" (1940) and "Two in One" (1954) could be considered as useful companion pieces to O'Brien's novels, but with their shape-shifting themes and absurdist techniques they also stand out as important examples of early postmodern fiction in their own right. Moreover, some of the later stories, such as "The Martyr's Crown" (1950) and "Donabate" (1952), offer fascinating insights into the interregnum between the two periods of O'Brien's novelistic output, i.e., between the exuberant novels of the early 1940s and the late, unexpected reprise in the early 1960s, which saw the publication of *The Hard Life* (1961) and *The Dalkey Archive* (1964). In these later stories and novels there is undoubtedly a shift in his aesthetic towards something slightly more realist, although the satirical focus remains consistent throughout. This contrarian impulse is still very much in evidence in his final unfinished novel, *Slattery's Sago Saga* (c.1964–66), which is included in the third section of this volume.

Overall, this anthology gathers together previously unavailable or dispersed material under one reader-friendly roof. However, given the multiplicity of names that O'Brien used (or is reputed to have used), this is by no means a definitive collection. Instead, we offer it up as an initial act of recovery rather than a completist project. Even so, it is clear to us that several of these stories deserve proper critical attention as important works within the general trajectory of international metafiction and the Irish literary tradition(s). Consequently, this volume is also an invitation to Flanneurs—both seasoned and fledgling—to find their own resonances and significances, not just within and between individual stories but in comparison with the more canonical novels and newspaper columns as well. In this respect, our own—possibly controversial—inclusion of John Shamus O'Donnell's "Naval Control" represents a speculative gesture designed to generate further discussion and discovery.

—Neil Murphy & Keith Hopper, Singapore and Oxford, 2013

A Note on the Texts

The stories in this collection are drawn from several periods and a variety of sources. In most cases, we have chosen to reproduce the earliest published versions available, and these base texts have been cross-checked against later versions published elsewhere. Where possible, we have also cross-checked the base texts against the original typescripts and manuscripts held at two archives: the Brian O'Nolan Papers, 1914–1966 (1/4/MSS 051), Special Collections Research Center, Morris Library, Southern Illinois University, Carbondale; and the Flann O'Brien Collection, 1881–1991 (MS97-27), Archives and Manuscripts, John J. Burns Library, Boston College.

Any significant variations between the base texts and other extant versions have been flagged, although some minor discrepancies and typographical errors have been silently sub-edited. The punctuation, which varies a little from story to story, has been standardised (em-dashes without spaces—for instance—is the preferred format, while we use three dots and a space for ellipses mid-sentence . . . and four dots for ellipses at the end of sentences. . . .). Throughout the volume, English and Hiberno-English spellings are used instead of the American forms.

A few cases merit specific mention. "John Duffy's Brother" was first published in Dublin in the *Irish Digest* (June 1940), and later in New York in *Story* (July–August 1941); however, we have chosen to use the original (undated) typescript version held at Boston College as our base text. The rationale for this is relatively straightforward (insofar as anything is ever straightforward when dealing with Flann O'Brien). In the American version, there is a reference to a character who "had gone to sea at the age of sixteen as a result of an incident arising out of an imperfect understanding of the sexual relation"; in the more prudish Irish version, this reads as "an imperfect understanding of the world." This says much about the draconian censorship code then in operation in Ireland—which O'Brien spent much of his career trying to subvert or circumvent—where anything signifying even the remotest sexual content was liable to be banned.[1] In turn, though, the American version has blandly smoothed out some of O'Brien's more idiosyncratic linguistic usages; for example, his pedantically precise description of a train's "four-wheel bogey" is changed to the more banal "four-wheel buggy." Consequently, we have decided that the Boston College typescript represented the cleanest copy available. (There is also an early draft typescript in the archive at Carbondale dated "2.12.1938"; however, this is incomplete and underdeveloped, so we did not incorporate it into the base text. Nonetheless, it remains a fascinating resource for future genetic scholars.)

In the case of O'Brien's unfinished novel, *Slattery's Sago Saga*, the most complete and mature version is the one first published in Claud Cockburn's *Flann O'Brien, Stories and Plays* (1973). However, we have re-edited this version in light of the original typescript held at Boston College (Cockburn, for all his recuperative virtues, sometimes has a rather heavy editorial hand). Unfortunately, that original typescript is incomplete, with three chapters having been mislaid. Therefore, this present text privileges the typescript version where possible, except for chapters two, three, and four, where we reproduce a slightly modified version of Cockburn's text. (There is also an early, largely handwritten version of *Slattery's Sago Saga* housed at Carbondale; we did not incorporate this manuscript into the base text as it is unreliably incomplete and largely underdeveloped.)

Sources and Resources

Brian Ó Nualláin, "Díoghaltais ar Ghallaibh 'sa Bhliain 2032," *Irish Press* (18 January 1932), pp. 4–5. Translated as "Revenge on the English in the Year 2032!" by Jack Fennell.

Brian Ó Nualláin, "Teacht agus Imtheacht Sheáin Bhuidhe," *Irish Press* (13 June 1932), p. 4. Translated as "The Arrival and Departure of John Bull" by Jack Fennell.

Brian Ó Nualláin, "Eachta an Fhir Ólta: CEOL!," *Irish Press*

[1] For a more detailed discussion of Irish literary censorship, see Keith Hopper, "The Dismemberment of Orpheus: Flann O'Brien and the Censorship Code," *Literature and Ethics: Questions of Responsibility in Literary Studies*, ed. Neil Murphy et al. (New York: Cambria Press, 2009), pp. 221–41.

(24 August 1932), p. 4. Translated as "The Tale of the Drunkard: MUSIC!" by Jack Fennell. Previously translated as "The Narrative of the Inebriated Man" by Breandán Ó Conaire in *Myles before Myles: A Selection of the Earlier Writings of Brian O'Nolan*, ed. John Wyse Jackson (London: Grafton, 1988), pp. 173–75.

Brian Ó Nualláin, "Mion-Tuairimí ár Sinnsir," *Irish Press* (29 September 1932), p. 4. Translated as "The Reckonings of Our Ancestors" by Jack Fennell.

Brian Ó Nualláin, "Aistear Pheadair Dhuibh," *Inisfail* 1.1 (March 1933), pp. 63-64. Translated as "The Tale of Black Peter" by Jack Fennell.

Brother Barnabas, "Scenes in a Novel," *Comhthrom Féinne* 8.2 (May 1934), pp. 29–30. Repr. *The Journal of Irish Literature* 3.1 (January 1974), special Flann O'Brien issue, ed. Anne Clissmann and David Powell (California: Proscenium, 1974), pp. 14-18; also repr. *Myles before Myles* (1983), pp. 77–81; and *Alive-Alive O!: Flann O'Brien's* At Swim-Two-Birds, ed. Rüdiger Imhof (Dublin: Wolfhound, 1985), pp. 34-38.

Flann O'Brien, "John Duffy's Brother," complete typescript (undated), box 3, folder 18, Flann O'Brien Collection, Boston College. There is also an early, incomplete typescript in the Carbondale archive dated "2.12.1938," although we have not used it in assembling our base text. "John Duffy's Brother" was first published in the *Irish Digest* (June 1940), pp. 69–73 (the byline describes it as being "From a Radio Éireann broadcast"). It was also published in *Story: The Magazine of the Short Story* [New York] 19.90 (July-August, 1941), pp. 65–68. As previously mentioned, there are minor (though interesting) variations between these two published versions. "John Duffy's Brother" was later reprinted in Flann O'Brien, *Stories and Plays*, ed. Claud Cockburn (1973; London: Grafton, 1986), pp. 89–97; and in *Black Water: The Anthology of Fantastic Literature*, ed. Alberto Manguel (London: Picador, 1983), pp. 371–76. There is also a short film version: *John Duffy's Brother*, directed by Mikel Murfi and adapted for the screen by Eoghan Nolan (Ireland: Park Films, 2006), 14 mins.

Flann O'Brien, "When I Met William of Orange," *Irish Digest* (April 1942), pp. 20–23. This is the published version of "Who Won the Battle of the Boyne? Or A Dialogue in Hades," the typescript of which is held at Boston College.

Lir O'Connor, "I'm Telling You No Lie!" *Irish Digest* (July 1943), pp. 15–18. The story in the *Irish Digest* is followed by an extract entitled "How to Play Poker," attributed to "Myles na gCopaleen in the *Irish Times*."

Myles na gCopaleen, "Drink and Time in Dublin," *Irish Writing: The Magazine of Contemporary Irish Literature*, no. 1 (1946), ed. David Marcus and Terence Smith, pp. 71–77. Repr. *1000 Years of Irish Prose*, ed. Vivian Mercier and David H. Greene (New York: Devin-Adair, 1952), pp. 509–15.

Brian Nolan, "The Martyr's Crown," *Envoy* 1.3 (February 1950), pp. 57–62. The original typescript (dated 1950), is logged as Brian O'Nolan / Myles na gCopaleen, "The Martyr's Crown," box 4, folder 1, Flann O'Brien Collection, Boston College. It was first reprinted in Flann O'Brien, *Stories and Plays* (1973), pp. 81–8. There is also a short film version: *The Martyr's Crown*, directed and adapted for the screen by Rory Bresnihan (Ireland: Park Films, 2007), 10 mins.

Myles na gCopaleen, "Donabate," *Irish Writing* 20-21 (November 1952), pp. 41-42; repr. *The Journal of Irish Literature* (1974), pp. 62–64.

Myles na Gopaleen, "Two in One," *The Bell* 19.8 (July 1954), pp. 30–34; repr. *The Journal of Irish Literature* (1974), pp. 56–61.

Brian O'Nolan, "After Hours," *Threshold* 21 (Summer 1967), pp. 15–18. This is reprinted here for the first time.

Flann O'Brien, *Slattery's Sago Saga, or From Under the Ground to the Top of the Trees*, unfinished novel, repr. Flann O'Brien, *Stories and Plays*, ed. Claud Cockburn (1973; London: Grafton, 1986), pp. 21–79. The original typescript of *Slattery's Sago Saga* is held at Boston College (box 3, folder 1; 55 pages, corrections in author's hand). This typescript is undated and has no title page or codified author, and three chapters are missing (chapters two, three, and four). There is also an early, largely handwritten version of *Slattery's Sago Saga* housed at the Carbondale archive (box 6, folder 1, "Book Reviews—a Holograph of 'Sago Saga'"), which is dated "15/12/64." A stage version of *Slattery's Sago Saga*, adapted by Arthur Riordan, was first performed by the Performance Corporation at Rathfarnham Castle, Dublin, on the 16th of July 2010, directed by Jo Mangan.

Brian O'Nolan / Flann O'Brien, "[For] Ireland Home & Beauty" (1940), box 4, folder 10, Brian O'Nolan Papers, Special Collections Research Center, Morris Library, Southern Illinois University, Carbondale. This typescript is an early draft version of "The Martyr's Crown" (1950), and is published here for the first time. The twelve-page typescript contains some handwritten emendations by O'Nolan, which we have marked up in our base text. This is not the most readable of formats, for which we apologise, but it does demonstrate how O'Nolan assiduously revised his own work.

John Shamus O'Donnell, "Naval Control," *Amazing Stories Quarterly* [USA] 5.1 (Winter 1932), pp. 141–43. This story, the provenance of which remains unproven, is reprinted here for the first time. Over to you, Dear Reader.

Acknowledgments

Initially, thanks are offered to John O'Brien and Jeremy M. Davies, of Dalkey Archive Press, for their steadfast support of this venture, and for their ongoing contribution to literature that matters. Thanks too to the School of Humanities and Social Sciences, NTU Singapore, for financial support that lead directly to this volume.

Several postgraduate students helped with early drafts of the individual stories, including Tansey Tang and Esther Ng; all of their work is greatly appreciated. Zhang Jieqiang worked as a research assistant on the later drafts, and his keen eye and meticulous editorial assistance were invaluable. Donal McCay and Paula Tebay offered useful commentary on some of the stories, and their readerly responses to "Naval Control" were particularly instructive.

Colleagues far and near have been crucial sounding-boards over the past few years, most notably Dr Daniel Jernigan, Prof Ondřej Pilný, Dr Jack Fennell, Dr Robert Lumsden, W. Michelle Wang, Annie Proulx, Aidan Higgins, Timothy O'Grady, Mikel Murfi, Eoghan Nolan, Dr Derek Hand, Dr Peter van de Kamp, Dr Joseph Brooker, Bernard O'Donoghue, Mick Henry, and Dr Jennika Baines, while Paul Fagan and Dr Ruben Borg of the International Flann O'Brien Society have been a great source of support and practical advice. Prof Joan Dean, Dr Carol Taaffe, John Wyse Jackson, Adam Winstanley, Dr Alana Gillespie, Marion Quirici and Adrian Naughton all provided important bibliographic information and materials, while Dr Seosamh Mac Muirí and Deirdre Learmont gave their expert advice on the stories in Irish. We are also very grateful to Eddie O'Kane for his wonderful artwork, and to David O'Kane for his visual expertise.

A special word of thanks is owed to Justine Sundaram, of the John J. Burns Library, Boston College, who was a constant source of support in very real, practical terms, despite numerous requests above and beyond the norm. Emma Wilcox, the English subject librarian at the School of Humanities and Social Sciences library, NTU, has, as always, been extremely supportive. Thanks, too, to David Chaplin and Astrid Fraser at St Clare's International College, Oxford, and to Prof Lance Pettitt and the Centre for Irish Studies at St Mary's University College, Twickenham.

Thanks are due to the Estate of Evelyn O'Nolan, for copyright permissions, and to Henry Thayer, at Brandt & Hochman Literary Agents, Inc., who currently represent the Estate in conjunction with A.M. Heath & Co., Ltd.

Deepest gratitude, as always, is offered to Niamh Moriarty and Su Salim Murphy for their practical support and encouragement.

Short Stories translated from the Irish (1932–33)

TEAĊT AGUS IMṪEAĊT ṠEÁIN ḂUIḊE

IARSMA AN ḂÉARLA

CUIREAḊ AN PLÁTAÍ CEOIL É !

BRIAN Ó NUALLÁIN

Translator's Note

The protean creature known variously as Brian Ó Nualláin, Brian O'Nolan, and Brian Nolan (amongst many others) spoke as many kinds of Irish as he had names. A native of Strabane in County Tyrone, he spent the first few years of his life in a household where nothing was spoken except Ulster Irish, and following the family's move to Dublin, he joined an education system in which Irish was held in a similar regard to Latin or Classical Greek—interesting, perhaps, but of no immediate relevance to the modern world, with a grammatical system and a vocabulary (drawn mostly from old poetry) indicative of the formal speech of a vanished aristocracy rather than a living vernacular. Ó Nualláin was an adolescent during the War of Independence (or the Anglo-Irish War, if you prefer), and became an adult as the country became a Free State. Having triumphed in a bitter Civil War, the Free State government pursued the restoration of the Irish language as a means to restore their own nationalist credibility, an effort that gave rise to a hotly contested "official standard" dialect (*an Caighdeán Oifigiúil*). In a very real sense, the Dáil (or principal chamber of the Irish parliament) was attempting to create a language by committee—a situation that positively begged to be savaged by a bilingual satirist.

In addition to his native dialect and the *Caighdeán Oifigiúil*, Ó Nualláin wrote in *Béarlachas* (English-inflected pidgin Gaelic) and deliberately bad Irish, and he was not above coining new phrases for comedic effect (see "The Arrival and Departure of John Bull" in this volume for some examples). In many cases, it is necessary to have Ó Nualláin's own grasp of the structure of the Irish language to understand a joke, and one of his favourite tricks was to write certain snippets of dialogue in Roman type, in short stories that were otherwise entirely printed in the government-approved "uncial" script. It is sometimes impossible not to lose a joke in translation, and explanatory footnotes do not really help.

In explaining the jokes, I have done Ó Nualláin's subtle humour a disservice, but in my defence, the Irish language is bristling with linguistic traps that prompt esoteric puns—for instance, the word "francach," written with a lowercase *f*, means "rat," but with a capital F, means "French" or "French person." The Irish equivalent for "There's no place like home" ("Níl aon tinteán mar do thinteáin féin," "There's no fireside like one's own fireside") is lampooned in a pun that insightfully comments on the subjective evaluation of one's own misfortune ("Níl aon tón tinn mar do thóin tinn féin," "There's no sore arse like one's own sore arse"). It can be a tricksy, slippery language, an ideal medium for a tricksy, slippery man like Ó Nualláin / O'Nolan / O'Brien. Trying to find the English for "Seacht nGeach" nearly drove me insane, and I owe a debt of gratitude to my teacher Seosamh Mac Muirí for helping me out on that one.

Seo é mo bhus—slán go fóill!

—Jack Fennell, University of Limerick, 2013

Revenge on the English in the Year 2032! (1932)

by Brian Ó Nualláin

With regard to the business of nourishment, the worldly man who earns his crust from the sweat of his brow more often experiences the lack of hunger than its excess, and it is true that this state of affairs is to be preferred; and it is also true that deliverance should be granted to the bag of bones who is empty but for the scrapings of the porridge-pot, or a couple of seed-potatoes with a drop of milk; but when a man is full to bursting point, he truly is in a sorry state. There is nothing left for him to do but fall into a deep sleep, with a powerful hope in him that he will find relief when he awakes.

Where Am I?

Thus it was for me, around Christmas, when this affliction, the disease of the bursting belly, came upon me and worked its mischief to render me insensible. Instead of going down to Hell or ascending to Heaven, as I had done many times before, I perceived that I was in a tightly packed place, on a cold, wide, sloping platform, packed from one end to the other by a horrible crowd of people that were slowly moving down the incline. After a long delay, shuffling and shoving, we reached another, more even platform, and the people spread out away from me a little. I put down the big heavy bag which I suddenly felt in my grasp, and I started fixing my cravat and staring about, trying to make sense of the scene around me.

Where in the world am I?, I wondered. Am I in Ireland or in Aran or in the deepest recesses of the devil's Hell? To my right I spotted a pious-looking priest tying his shoelaces, and that settled the case about Hell, but I was looking and listening for another while yet before I realised that I was standing on a harbour.

I Came Aboard a Ship

"It's likely," I said to myself, "that I just came off that ship." But, dear reader, what a ship! It was a narrow, streamlined, elegant vessel that was resting in the water, shivering and trembling as though she was impatient to be released back out onto the deep, slicing through the waves and charging off on her way, just like a hound on the hunt, seizing the wind before her and racing ahead of the gale behind. . . .

Ah, a thousand pities seven times over, gentle reader! How empty and miserly is the language of today, when we try to speak of unearthly wonder! There is neither oratory in the mouth nor literature in the pen for it, and even if there were, neither would suffice in this particular instance.

I was startled when I noticed a vicious little busybody opening my bag, trying, or so I thought, to steal my night-clothes.

"Well now!" I said, giving him a little kick in the ankle. He saw the temper on me and raised his head.

"Do you have any whiskey?" he asked.

"The saints in Heaven know that there's a shortage of spirits going on," I said, sniggering. "But that whole business is behind me now for a long time. I'd love a little glass just now, all the same: never before in my life have my senses been so deranged!"

A Hundred Years Hence!

"You have to pay five shillings on this hat," he said, pulling a new hat out of the depths of the bag. I paid the money without saying a word, and he gave me a receipt; I looked at it, and the date filled me with astonishment—*12/02/2032.*

"I thought," I said, "that it was only the eleventh."

I picked up my bag. I felt those people moving over yonder towards the long electric train that was standing near us; I pushed myself over, with great struggling and shoving, and I was about to board when I realised that someone behind me was trying to catch my attention. I turned, and I saw a small, low fellow, as broad as three men, a sharp, bitter face on him, and a strange squareness to his shoulders that brought the image of a bull to mind. An Englishman, I said to myself, if God ever created one. He spoke, and I knew from his accent and his words that I was correct.

An Englishman, To Be Sure

"*Excuse me,*" he said shyly, "*but do you speak English?*"[1]

"I do indeed," I said politely, answering in English. "If you need my assistance or my counsel, you shall have them in abundance."

"*Well, I'm in a bit of a hole,*" he said timidly. "*You see, not speaking your beastly language here, I am rather at sea. I meant to buy a phrase-book before I left Holyhead, but I forgot about it in the rush of getting away—and here I am. Not one of these officials knows what the dickens I'm talking about. What I want to know is the address of an English-speaking hotel—in Blaclee—is that right?*"[2]

"Hmm," I said. "That's not so bad. I believe there is at least one person who speaks English in every hotel in the city. I have a little phrasebook I picked up on the ship. You're welcome to it." I gave it to him:

> PHRASEBOOK
>
> Suitable, appropriate and expedient for the use of the foreigner, includes:
>
> - Gaelic songs and airs
> - Gaelic phrases
> - Ulster Gaelic phrases
>
> With reference to the everyday lives of the people in every district, diocese and parish of Ireland.
>
> Price: Gandailín / threepence / half-*réal*.[3]

The little Englishman opened the book. I recognised from his gloomy expression and his twisted mouth that Gaelic was not coming to him easily. Not that surprising, I supposed. I looked around to see who else was in the carriage with us. There was a bulging, haughty-looking man in the corner opposite me, boasting to two

[1] Translator's Note: The original story was published in Gaelic uncial script, except for the parts spoken by the tourist. This joke is lost when the entire narrative is rendered in Roman type.

[2] The tourist is mispronouncing "Baile Átha Cliath," the Gaelic name for Dublin.

[3] "Gandailín" means "little gander," and is probably a reference to an Irish coin of the future. From 1928 to the introduction of the euro in 2002, Irish coinage featured particular animals—horse, bull, hen, hare, salmon, pig, woodcock and wolfhound—rather than heads of state or other symbols. The obverse to all of these coins was a harp.

women of the wondrous things he had done in London, and next to me there was a pair of young men playing cards and gossiping about some marriage that did not work out. Sitting in front of me was my English student, who was now shaking and laughing with relief.

Speaking Gaelic

The train moved quickly along on its journey and after a little while, the Englishman looked up and said:

"I am in need of, I want, I require, food, food, food!"[4]

"Aha!" said I. My God, who ever heard a proclamation like that before!

"How are you? How are things? How's tricks?"

"Well, well, and well," I replied, in spite of myself.

"I awoke, I woke up, I arose at seven o'clock, my boy, my lad, my buck!"

"Well, well, well," I said.

"Where is the public house, the pub, the nearest and closest and least-far-away church. I am a Protestant, Catholic, Jewish Scottish Orangeman! . . . *How's that?*"

"Well now," I said, speaking in English, "that's not too bad at all. Don't try too hard to vocalise the 'ch' sound: at the moment, you'll only burst your larynx. You've got a good bit of Gaelic already, and you're well able for it. Keep at it, and may it work out for you."

The Treachery of the English

"*Thanks*," he said. He opened the book again and started studying. I took out my pipe, lit it, and turned my attention to the estimation and examination of the foreigner.

"Englishman"! That one word put thousands of thoughts spilling into my mind; I thought of the insult and injury that had been done to the Gaels by Diarmaid Mac Murchadha,[5] and from then after—the English lords murdering Gaels and stealing their land. The broken Treaty of Limerick, the laws against the Faith—the death of Gaelic and

---

[4] In the original, the Englishman briefly starts speaking Gaelic (and in uncial script) at this point.

[5] A deposed King of Leinster, who pledged allegiance to King Henry II of England in exchange for military support to reclaim his crown, thus triggering the Norman invasion of Ireland in 1171.

its hard, agonising rebirth, and to top it all off, the shameful deed that was done when 2,000 respectable Corkmen were killed in Dublin on Halloween, 1997, by the machinations of the British Government.

A sudden fit of anger and hatred hit me; I turned to John Bull, and spoke to him:

Teaching the Profanities

"I'm just after remembering," I said in English, "that there's a British Hotel in the city, and nothing is spoken there but your own English. When we reach the city, take your bag to the first taxi you see, and say to the driver—well, say these words. . . ."

I have no desire, fair reader, to publish the words I taught to him: but I don't mind telling you that no earthly ear has ever heard a stream of talk so full of malevolence, of ancient, awful, filthy and sour maledictions, of dark, vexed, intemperate curses, and tremendous oaths so vile they could make a corpse walk again. Never before was such a despicable monologue composed.

The two of us worked so hard, me instructing and him memorising, that he had a respectable grasp of the speech long before we reached our destination.

All that's left now is to pin the tail on my story. When the train stopped, I waved John Bull a hurried goodbye, took off out of his sight, hid behind a wall and focused my two eyes on him. Yer man picked up his bags, hastened to a taxi, put down his luggage and turned to the driver.

What Happened Then

His back was to me, so I was not able to determine when he started, or if the talk was coming to him easily. But I saw that there was a bright blush spreading across the back of his neck and, it seemed to me, that he was emphasising his recitation with hand gestures, putting great energy and exertion into it. An ominous change came over the face of the taxi driver, who looked as though rage was taking hold of him; even though the driver was obviously offended, it seemed that John Bull managed to get halfway through a second recitation of the spiel before the driver launched into a furious attack on him, and it seemed to me that I had better be on my way.

As I departed, I glanced over my shoulder, and I saw that my student was in the custody of a big, Gaelic Garda: and sure as Easter falls on a Sunday, I knew that Garda was a Corkman.

That's how it happened, good reader; and if my story warrants a postscript, here's one for you: if Diarmaid Mac Murchadha played a dreadful trick on the Gaels, the Gaels have never been slow to give a little beating to Diarmaid's friends, if God grants them the opportunity!

The Arrival and Departure of John Bull: The Relic of English—Let it Be Put on Record! (1932)[1]

by Brian Ó Nualláin

I recently found this bizarre epic beneath the floor of a house that was being demolished on Tara Street, Dublin, as the street was being widened. We have no knowledge of the author or his people, but it seems this story concerns the world of tomorrow rather than the ancient past. Not everything in this story is as unbelievable as it may seem.

On an assembly day, when the high-council was convened by Seán Mac Cumhaill, son of Airt son of Tréanmhóir of the Lineage of Baoisgne, and the seven tribes of the Gaels and the seven tribes of the Common Gaels[2] were gathered in Dun Laoghaire, they cast their eyes on the tide and the wide open sea, and it was not long before they saw, coming directly from the east, a speedy, scurrying boat with full sails, swiftly scudding across the surging, surly seas,[3] in towards the land.

The Giant

As that big wide ship came ashore and its sails were taken down, the nobles of Ireland expected masses, multitudes and militias to come charging out of her, but they saw but one warrior—a tall, brawny, twisted man, misshapen, murderous, malformed, crooked-toothed and monstrous, and he slowly, sluggishly, wearily coming in from the ship to the beautiful shores of Éireann, coming to attack Seán Mac Cumhaill and the nobles of Ireland.

Fleeing Before Him

[1] Translator's Note: This is the first indication that Ó Nualláin is deliberately using poor Irish in this text: the phrase used for "record" in this case is "plátaí ceoil," which literally means "music plates."

[2] The phrase used throughout the text is "Gnáth-Gaedheal." "Gnáth" means "common" or "usual," but it could also be used to mean "habitual," perhaps implying that the "Gnáth-Gaedheal" could be "Gaels by Custom or Habit," i.e. citizens of non-Gaelic heritage.

[3] In the original text, the adjective used to describe the seas is "mí-chéillidhe," which I have translated here as "surly" but whose meaning is closer to "insane, stupid or insensible."

That's what Seán and the nobles were thinking, anyway, as they saw this giant coming towards them. Wonder and revulsion overtook them at the sight of him, and they rose to their feet, pulled their livery and armour on over their bare thighs and buttocks, and departed quickly and swiftly; they went quick-footed[4] on their way, mad for road; they departed in a mass migration and stampede; and proceeded, nimbly, boldly, speedily, and witlessly, without cease nor delay, to the obscure unknown cities and to the tangled, knotty dark forests: and to every other place that could provide shelter in the kingdom of Dublin.

DAISIES!

However, the opposing warrior continued to rush straight on, sprinting after Seán and all of his companions, and it was not long before he reached the end of his journey, and he came into the presence of Seán and the brave, steadfast men of Éireann (as many of them as were in that spot at the time, anyway), right in the dim, misty centre of the wood.[5] Beautiful Seán Mac Cumhaill was at that time deftly, dextrously, daintily gathering daisies, and putting them together in the form of a chain, whistling gently and sweetly all the while.

I WILL STAY!

Indeed, when he saw the strange giant coming at him, a swell of wonder and anxiety[6] seized him, he blessed him with words lavish, lofty and lionhearted, inquired after his health and well-being, and gave him leave for lecturing, speechifying, and oratory. The giant grumpily beheld Seán and all his companions, bared his protracted, primitive, pointy teeth, moved his grisly, grimy gums, and spoke:

"O King of the Gaels!" said he, hardly, bitterly, and without humility.

"Seán Mac Cumhaill, son of Airt son of Tréanmhóir of the Lineage of Baoisgne is my name," replied the vigorous leader of the

[4] Here, Ó Nualláin uses "troigh" to denote "foot," when it actually means a foot *in length*.

[5] "Coilleadh," meaning "castration," is used instead of the homophone "coille," meaning "woods" or "forest."

[6] The indicated word is "aithis," meaning "reproach" or "shame"; however, the word used is "áthas," meaning joy.

Gaels.

"'Sean'?" said the giant.

"No, actually," Seán said, having perceived the Roman print, "it's *Seán*."[7]

"*John Bull* is my name," the giant responded.

"The best thing for you to do now," Seán Mac Cumhaill said, "is to take yourself back to whichever region of the world you came from."

"It is true that I will not," the giant said, sneering, "but I will remain in this place as long as I have the will and the desire to do so."

"I have never been in the habit," Seán said, "of socialising or co-habiting in the same spot with the likes of you, and I'm not about to start doing so now."

"Exactly, well said!" said one of the Gaelic noblemen in the depths of the woods, clapping.

"I beg to differ," said John Bull.

"Well, now," said another Gael in the depths of the woods.

What He Wants

"I am John Bull," the giant announced, boldly and fervently, "and as much of the world as I have walked since departing my homeland, I have thus far not left one country, atoll, or island without demanding tribute from them, or bringing them beneath the dominion of my excise duties and the abject slavery of my tariffs: and it is my desire for the dominion and taxation of this territory to be mine as well, along with the misery of all its people, and to bring Gaelic poverty and servitude to the seven tribes of the Gaels and to the seven tribes of the Common Gaels with the heavy axe of those tariffs; *that* is my ambition for this kingdom."

"I understand," replied Seán Mac Cumhaill, leader of the Gaels.

A Man with English!

"That being said," the repulsive mongrel of a giant continued, "if

[7] Originally, the story was printed in the Irish uncial alphabet, except for certain phrases spoken by the giant, which were printed in Roman type. Note the absence of an accent over the 'a' in Seán's name as the giant pronounces it.

any of your heroes can be troubled to prove to me that Gaelic has great literature, or that there is one courageous, cultivated, clever, courtly, courteous, consummate author among you, or that the noble, ancient tongue of the Saxon is alive, however much of it is left, in some corner of Ireland, I will not do one thing more to trouble ye, but take myself back to my own land without delay."

"We have as many great authors and great works as you'd like."

"Recite the titles for me," the giant said.

"There's *Yesterday and Today*," said Seán Mac Cumhaill, "and *Heavy and Light*."

"There's *Dusk and Dawn*," said another Gaelic noble.

"There's *Old and New*," another Gael said.

"There's *Day and Night*."

"There's *Love and Gloom*."[8]

"If that's the case," said the giant, "then it seems that all those well-read works are somewhat formulaic. The fact is that is ye now have to prove that ye have Anglo-Saxon somewhere right now, or become a people without a kingdom."

THE HUNT

"I understand[9] all you have said," replied Seán Mac Cumhaill, the Gaelic supreme leader.

It was then that Seán asked of the multitude around and beside him who among them would undertake the great expedition and thoroughly search Ireland, without rest or respite, until Gaelic masters were found who were skilled in the English dialect. Two fleet-footed, valorous, manly men, Peadar Shamuseen Pat's Mary and Black Mickey Donnell, emerged from the horde of Gaels hiding in the deep woods, and went to the side of Seán Mac Cumhaill, supreme leader of the Gaels, and before long they departed as fast as they could on the wide plains road through Ireland. John Bull made a coarse, cackling laugh, and sat down on a stone.

[8] The titles on this list are all real. In order: *Indé agus Indiu* by Seán Mac Meanman; *Trom agus Eadtrom* by Mícheál Breathnach; *Ciot is Dealán* by Séamus Ó Grianna; *Sean Agus Nua* by Gearóid Ó Nualláin; *Lá agus Oidhche* by Micheál Mac Liammóir; and A*n Grádh agus an Ghruaim*, by Seosamh Mac Grianna.

[9] The word used throughout the text is "deontach," meaning "voluntary, in agreement, content or willing."

There's Four of Them!

It was not long after the departure of Peadar and Mickey, the two bold heroes, that they returned to the presence of Seán Mac Cumhaill and John Bull, and four elderly men in their company, coming along feebly, slowly and reluctantly. Seán Mac Cumhaill blessed them gracefully with sweet gentle words, and gave them leave to commence lecturing and orating and speechifying. John Bull gave a coarse sniggering laugh, and said:

"If you have English, speak it!"

It was then that Mickey and Peadar explained that the elderly men were from Belfast, Dublin, Cork, and Limerick, and that varying degrees of the dialect of the Saxons yet remained on their tongues.

"This is the well-read learned gentleman from Belfast," he said, "and his name is in the mouths of seers and storytellers, and the readers of poems and books and useful descriptions, all over the world. Recite your bit, Eoghan. Recite to us the English you have!"

The wise, civil old man opened his mouth and said:

The Speech of the Men

"*Not an inch. Used as a pawn in the game. Up the Twalfth. To aitch with the Pee.*" That was as much as he had. Joy and wonderment came over John Bull. Then, the elderly gent from Dublin spoke all that he knew.

"*Alf. Where were you in sixteen? O Yeah! Sez me! Branch-a Map-aíochta & Survey-reachta.*" Then it was the Corkman's turn to speak; he had naught but a strange scrap that he did not understand himself:

"*Dep. Cork 9.25. Arr. Dublin 12.35.*
Dep. Cork 1.30. Arr. Dublin 4.16.
No Return Tickets issued."

It was then that the learned expert from Limerick spoke, and he had only one English sentence:

"*Sprechen Sie Deutsch.*"

John Bull, when heard this melodious talk, was seized by a surge of joy: he sent for his servant, and put the same sweet talk on music-plates with help from Conradh an Bhéarla:[10] and John Bull put his hand on the hand of Seán Mac Cumhaill, and they feasted and celebrated for a month and a day, and then John Bull returned to his own kingdom. Everything hitherto was the tale of Seán Mac Cumhaill.

[10] "The Covenant of English." This is a parody of *Conradh na Gaeilge*, Douglas Hyde's initiative to restore the Irish language.

The Tale of the Drunkard: MUSIC! (1932)

by Brian Ó Nualláin

He was a small, inoffensive, level-headed man, and I would not make note of that latter characteristic except that he was speaking angrily to a street-lamp. He was drunk, it seemed to me, and the right thing to do would be to direct him homewards. I glanced at him.

"What is the meaning of this? What's wrong with you!" I said. "It'd be more in your line to be in bed, instead of staggering around drunk all over the city like this. You'd be better off if you turned your back on the drink, and your face to the fireplace—an intelligent, mild-mannered man such as yourself—and took up another hobby, like fretwork, or listening to the gramophone. . . ."

"GRAMOPHONE!" He regarded me with two eyes containing the savagery of Hell—two venomous, red embers.

The Drunkard's Story

"Stay for a moment," he said, "until I tell you my story. It'll depress you, if you're a normal man at all. . . . One airy Spring morning ten years ago, I heard the woman's voice for the first time, and if my memory is not deranged, I reckoned at the time that she had a good voice, a voice that would become first-rate with care and practice.

"It seems that there was an ambition of the same kind in that girl's heart, for the practice was started the very next day and it continued, without restraint or pause, without respite or delay, for the next ten years. I'm still here, but alas, I'm not the same man I was back then. . . . I had an almighty craving for music at that time, and I'm not saying I never lifted a fiddle the odd time in the loneliness of night—God forgive me."

The Woman with One Tune

"But yer wan over. She lived in the house opposite my own, across the street. 'Annie Laurie' was the first sound I heard as I woke up, and 'Annie Laurie' was the last note that broke my heart and I drifting off to sleep; and the clock chimed Annie-Laurie-Annie-Laurie until morning. 'Gloom follows after glee.' Well, the glee was across the way from dawn to dusk, and it was myself who got the gloom, the mood swings, the nervous frenzies, the fits of anger, the malice. The thought of slashing my own throat was sweeter to me than those merry words, 'Annie Laurie.'

"If the situation went on any longer in the same way, I knew that nostalgia and loneliness would creep into my soul, that I would become heartsick and short of wits. What happened then? I was in the middle of shaving one morning when I realised that there was another tune being played. I said to myself, that nice decent girl has a new song—fair play to her, she's improving."

THE MAN'S VOICE

"Then, I realised that it was a man's voice. Down the stairs with me. The music was coming from the house right next to mine, on the right-hand side. The song ended, and a voice then said that we were 'going over to the Royal Hotel, Blackpool, for dance music.' And we went. . . . And stately and low, but growing more powerful with every passing moment, a high female voice proclaimed that Maxwelton Braes were 'bonn-ee.'

"A year went by, and the situation changed again. There was another house just next to mine, on the left-hand side, and one morning I perceived, over the din of 'Annie Laurie' and the racket of the other man, someone announcing to the world that a distinguished guest was about to give a 'Talk' on 'The Decoration of the Modern Sitting-room.'

"More time went by. Annie Laurie was still alive, so lively that I supposed that the flower of second youth was upon her. Daventry was coming in at its very best on one side, and Radio Paris was steering the revelry on the other. A barrel organ could be heard constantly in that neighbourhood, that and a piper whose ears and pipes are far from being in tune, unknown to him. . . ."

"TALKS"

"Faith," I said, "that's an awful state of affairs. What did you do?"

"A story with no good in it, without a doubt. I wrote to the Minister for Posts and Telegraphs. He said that he had a plan. 'Talks' would be broadcast, advising the public, that would bring about an improvement in my situation. Maybe. 'TALKS' my granny! I said. I fetched a long, sharp knife, and I murdered the two men who were so fond of the radio (and one of those poor lads with eight children). I was about to dispatch 'Annie Laurie' to her eternal rest, when I remembered it was time for me to be on my way to the Congress at Lausanne."

"The Congress?"

"Yeah. Don't you recognise me? I'm Napoleon Bonaparte!"

"Begob, you're right," said I, panicking a little.

"Wait 'til you see my lovely knife." The red eyes were twinkling like the stars on Halloween night.

"I'll have a look at it tomorrow," I said, striding away with my best foot forward.

The Reckonings of our Ancestors (1932)
by Brian Ó Nualláin

Below is a selection from a bundle of papers recently found hidden inside one of the walls of the National Library, as those same walls were being demolished, repaired and renovated by men from the Office of Public Works in Dublin. It is believed that these papers were wrapped around the lunch of a workman hundreds of years ago, when the walls of the library were first being constructed, and that they were sealed inside the wall by accident. This theory is confirmed by the stench of fish and chips on the paper.

As regards the writing itself, it is clear that it is a selection of letters which were sent to a leading newspaper or magazine long ago; we do not know its name, however, and there is no information on it to be found in the old books at all.

The text has been fully edited, abbreviations have been expanded, and all instances of Old Irish have been translated to clear New Irish.

*

Dear Sir,

One night when myself and my mates here in Almhuin were together in the one assembly and in the one spot and in one sleeping-place, having chased, hunted, and slaughtered across the hills, gentle grasslands, and woodlands of Éireann, it was clear and evident to us that we would not be allowed our sleep, or permitted to remedy our exhaustion, for there were huge crowds and gangs of corner-boys out on the street at strange, occult hours of the night, playing football and "The Scotsman's Leap" [hopscotch], and hallooing, with bonfires and tremendous roaring.

When my companions and I tried to converse with some of them, furthermore, they responded with reproach and dire insults, and said they were the quietest and most peaceful crowd you could hope for.

Where are the Guards? The High King?

—With great respect,

Fionn Mac Cumhaill Mac A., etc.

*

My dear friend,

In Doire an Chairn the other afternoon, I heard a blackbird singing. I believe this is the first time I have heard it so early in the year. Do any other readers have similar stories?

—Yours etc.,

Fhlaithbheartach Mac Colla, poet.[1]

*

Amiable master,

I went from Baile Gréine to Sliabh Fhuaith by chariot, and for that journey, the charioteer demanded two bags of flour, a silk cloak, and two bronze pots. Isn't it time that a stop was put to this kind of blaggarding?

—Yours,

"Totally Disgusted."

*

Sir,

It is with permission and with great delight that I put before the Gaelic public a summary of the letters that we have sent to the two overseas kingdoms conquered by the King of Ireland, i.e., the Kingdom of the Saxons and the Kingdom of the Dalriada in Scotland, in response to communications received from them asking for an alleviation or relief of their taxes. This is a copy of the letter, translated into the sweet, verbose English of the Saxons by our clever, knowledgeable poets:

"*Gentlemen,*

Take a victory and a blessing! The Government have considered the contents of your letter dated 3rd ult. and regret that an adjustment of the financial relations between the three independent and self-governing

[1] Translator's Note: This refers to the poem "Lon Doire an Chairn" by the eighteenth-century poet Peadar Ó Doirnín, translated as "The Blackbird of Derrycairn" (1943) by Austin Clarke.

members of the Gaelic Commonwealth is not at the moment feasible owing to a variety of diverse and intricate difficulties in the sphere of world economics resultant on the prevailing depression, the successful solving of which will provide the only basis for further negotiation.

We feel sure, however, that with the dawning of a brighter era and with the adjustment of the world polity for the general benefit of the human race, with a striving for mutual understanding and amicable relations, with the coming of a spiritual as well as an economic unity between our peoples geographically and politically united by the grace of Providence, with the spreading of good-will and universal brotherhood, with the dawning of a new and brighter era of mutual understanding and friendly intercourse, coupled with a firm realisation that the great destiny of the independent States are inseparably linked, each with the other—all of which are easily attainable in the realms of statesmanship—a better and brighter era of mutual understanding and mutual advantage will be dawning."[2]

—Cormac, Son of Art.

Del. Gra. Er. Omn. Rex. Fid. Def. Eng.-Scot. Imp.

*

Dear Friend,

My son is being obliged to spend most of his time at school learning this "Compulsory English," instead of studying poetry or magic. What will he gain from English when he leaves the country? Not one note is spoken in Scotland other than Gaelic, and the Kingdom of the Saxons is full of nobody but violent, ignorant savages; Gaelic is spoken throughout two thirds of the world—or are we to believe that there are other countries somewhere out there? Bah!

—Yours,

"Anti-Humbug."

*

Good Master,

When are the King's Guards going do something about the gurriers that are constantly throwing stones in Almhain-slim-na-sleagh-

[2] The original text is in Gaelic uncial script, except for this section which is in Roman.

séim? The skins on two of my windows were punctured a couple of days ago.

—Pro Bono Publico,

Latin Scribe.

P.S. My card is enclosed.

*

Honest exemplar,

I have an excellent violin, and there is delicate writing inside it saying "A. Stradivarius fecit 381 A.D." Can any reader out there tell me whether this violin is worth five hundred bags of flour?

—Bacrach Draoi

*

My good man,

I would like to let the public know through your valuable column that there is no connection between myself and the man named Feidhlimidh Fuar na Feamnaighe arrested by the King's Guards for stealing potatoes in beautiful Almhain. Thanking you in advance,

With great respect,

Feidhlimidh Fuar na Feamnaighe.

The Tale of Black Peter (1933)

by Brian Ó Nualláin

Black Peter was born in a little white cottage in the middle of the Bog between the mountains and the sea; the kind of cottage you would see if you took the road back from Cheap a' Mhadaidh and you heading for Alt a' Chait—a lovely little lime-washed house, sitting comfortably by itself in the centre of the valley. To be sure, there is no valley at Cheap a' Mhadaidh, nor at Cúl an Bhobaire or Chros-bealaigh or Cúig nGeach either; there's nothing there but Bog.[1] Regardless, this was the kind of house a true Gaeilgeoir always sees in a mountain glen and he taking the road back.

There was no blind old storyteller living there (as there should have been), but, as I said above, only Black Peter and his mother, a widow with a good span of years behind her.

One morning, as the infant Peter was playing among the ashes and slowly coming into full possession of his faculties and speech, he gathered his courage, sped across the floor and stared out onto his native land. He saw the surly dun Bog stretching back to where the sky met the earth.

"God help us," Peter said, "the world is brown."

The seasons came and went, and the day arrived when Peter stood on his own two feet. He would often head out piling and gathering on the Bog around his cottage; he would pick up a hard, prickly sod of turf here, a soft wet one there, and he knocked great sport out of this collecting. Strange little flowers, too, and sticks and big lumps of Bog pine. He would bring the whole lot back to his mother, and indeed there was often a beating waiting for him instead of thanks for his labours.

Several times his mother set him on her knee, when the gloomy black clouds of the night were drawing down their mantle, and the salty spray of the sea blowing melancholy clouds of fog in across the Bog.

"Peter," she would say, "always be friendly to the Bog, be good to it and be charitable. If you are a friend to it, there won't be a jot

[1] Translator's Note: The place-names, in order, translate as "The Dog's Lawn," "The Cat's Ravine," "The Back of the Trickster," "Cross-road," and "The Five Geese."

of treachery waiting for you out there, and it will do no harm to you for the whole of your life. But may the saints in Heaven help you should you ever lose the Bog's friendship. That which could be your best friend, can also be your worst enemy. The Bog has a long memory. . . ."

*

The years went by and Black Peter grew up. He left the doorstep behind and walked the main road that twisted and turned around the Bog. He experienced new things in the wider world: bare rocks; watchful, authoritative men with big black hats on them; other cottages and public houses; the seashore and waves and fishing. . . . It was not long before he was as bold and loud-mouthed as any of the natives.

It's no great matter to say that he spent every other night staying up late, watching the *seanchaí*-man in the corner and he throwing his two flat feet into the embers, lighting his pipe, clearing his throat, and starting into stories of the Fianna. There was no better storyteller than him from east to west, and he was renowned from the heavens to Aran. Sometimes there would be a *céilidhe*, the mighty, spirited men dancing with the neat, laughing girls; and those who weren't dancing were secretly drinking *poitín* behind a wall in the dusk. The poitín would always be kept in a five-naggin bottle, and that bottle would be kept in a hole in the wall. Once a week without fail, two men would come over from Bárr na Blagaide,[2] one of them trying to propose marriage to Máire, the daughter of the publican. Máire would always be asleep, but when her father and the visitors had downed a couple of glasses of poitín in her honour, he would call for her —Wake up, Máire —Who's below —Paddy Mickey and Mickey Paddy —I wouldn't take him if he was the last man in Ireland —He's a decent, kind man, and he has a fine parcel of land —I don't care —Get dressed and come down here at once, my love . . . and Máire would come down and take him as a husband, after a lot of negotiation.

Other nights, Peter would go walking along the beach. In summer or in winter, it was always a stormy night when Peter went out walk-

[2] "Bárr na Blagaide" means "Bald Man's Peak."

ing, and the poor fishermen out on the choppy mouth of the bay, in the throes of death. Their mothers and wives would be crying and wailing on the shore, soaked to the marrow with the spray of the sea, looking on in torment at the unfortunate men out among the seaweed, their boats broken in the water, and they trying to come ashore. Peter saw the same bold man go into the sea with the same cable to help the fishermen, the same women trying to talk sense into him and keening that another poor man was lost. . . . Other times, he would go waking the dead (or people would die suddenly and frequently all over the Bog), he would pray, take a pinch of snuff, and drink poitín, and hear the revelry and the tumult of voices next door.

"DAMN IT!" said Peter, in loud and clear voice.

He said that often.

A day came when Peter arose early in the morning and put on his Aran jumper and his woollen rags. He ate a bowl of stirabout and twelve nettles, lovely nourishing nettles of the kind that do be on the Bog. He said a mouthful of his regular prayers. Then he leaped vigorously over the half-door and raced across the Bog in a raging temper, and he did not break his stride until he reached the house of Father Séamus. He woke the priest.

"God and Mary and Patrick be with you this morning."

"God and Mary and Patrick and Brigid be with you," Peter replied. "I have an important question for you. Tell me this much: WHO CREATED ME AND THIS MISERABLE COUNTRY?"

"God didn't create it," the priest answered. "It was Parthalán Mac an Dubhdha, author, and Feidhlimídh Ó Casaidhe, poet—both natives of Dublin. . . ."

Peter did not say another word, but grabbed a fine heavy double-barrelled shotgun that was hanging on the wall, secreted it under his coat and departed without delay. He headed south as the day was dawning, and disappeared into the mists of the Bog.

He was never heard from again, but it was said that there was some bad business done in Dublin.

*

The Bog is still there, but the 'b' is small now. Father Séamus says it's not as brown as it used to be, and that it's going black in some places, but there is grass growing on it now, and barley and potatoes and peas as well. The storyteller is silent, the fishermen are safe, and the women are on top of the business of keeping the embers and ashes in the fireplace. Máire is married and dissatisfied.

As well as that, there are shops on the bog now, selling bus-tickets and cigarettes and the *Daily Mail*.[3] There are ordinary people on the bog today, who have never heard the tale of Black Peter.

[3] "Bus-ticket," "cigarette" and "daily mail" [sic] all appear in English in the original text. In other early short works, Ó Nualláin would contrast the two languages by making use of two different typefaces—uncial for Gaelic, and Roman for English. This story, however, was originally published entirely in Roman type, detracting from the recurring joke.

Short Stories in English (1934–67)

Scenes in a Novel (1934)

by Brother Barnabas

(Probably Posthumous)

I am penning these lines, dear reader, under conditions of great emotional stress, being engaged, as I am, in the composition of a posthumous article. The great blots of sweat which gather on my brow are instantly decanted into a big red handkerchief, though I know the practice is ruinous to the complexion, having regard to the open pores and the poisonous vegetable dyes that are used nowadays in the Japanese sweat-shops. By the time these lines are in neat rows of print, with no damn over-lapping at the edges, the writer will be in Kingdom Come.* (See Gaelic quotation in 8-point footnote.) I have rented Trotsky's villa in Paris, though there are four defects in the lease (three reckoning by British law) and the drains are—what shall I say?—just a *leetle* bit Gallic. Last week, I set about the melancholy task of selling up my little home. Auction followed auction. Priceless books went for a mere song, and invaluable songs, many of them of my own composition, were ruthlessly exchanged for loads of books. Stomach-pumps and stallions went for next to nothing, whilst my ingenious home-made typewriter, in perfect order except for two faulty characters, was knocked down for four and tuppence. I was finally stripped of all my possessions, except for a few old articles of clothing upon which I had waggishly placed an enormous reserve price. I was in some doubt about a dappled dressing-gown of red fustian, bordered with a pleasing grey piping. I finally decided to present it to the Nation. The Nation, however, acting through one of its accredited Sanitary Inspectors, declined the gift—rather churlishly I thought—and pleading certain statutory prerogatives, caused the thing to be burnt in a yard off Chatham Street within a stone's

*"Truagh sin, a leabhair bhig bháin
Tiocfaidh lá, is ba fíor,
Déarfaidh neach os cionn do chláir
Ní mhaireann an lámh do scríobh."

["It is a pity, beloved little book
A day will come, to be sure,
Someone will inscribe over your contents
'The hand that wrote this lives not.'" (Trans. Jack Fennell)]

throw of the house where the Brothers Sheares played their last game of *taiplis* [draughts]. Think of that! When such things come to pass, as Walt Whitman says, you re-examine philosophies and religions. Suggestions as to compensation were pooh-poohed and sallies were made touching on the compulsory acquisition of slum property. You see? If a great mind is to be rotted and deranged, no meanness or no outrage is too despicable, no maggot of officialdom is too contemptible to perpetrate it . . . the ash of my dressing-gown, a sickly wheaten colour, and indeed, the whole incident reminded me forcibly of Carruthers McDaid.† Carruthers McDaid is a man I created one night when I had swallowed nine stouts and felt vaguely blasphemous. I gave him a good but worn-out mother and an industrious father, and coolly negativing fifty years of eugenics, made him a worthless scoundrel, a betrayer of women and a secret drinker. He had a sickly wheaten head, the watery blue eyes of the weakling. For if the truth must be told I had started to compose a novel and McDaid was the kernel or the fulcrum of it. Some writers have started with a good and noble hero and traced his weakening, his degradation and his eventual downfall; others have introduced a degenerate villain to be ennobled and uplifted to the tune of twenty-two chapters, usually at the hands of a woman—"She was not beautiful, but a shortened nose, a slightly crooked mouth and eyes that seemed brimful of a simple complexity seemed to spell a curious attraction, an inexplicable charm." In my own case, McDaid, starting off as a rank waster and a rotter, was meant to sink slowly to absolutely the last extremities of human degradation. Nothing, absolutely nothing, was to be too low for him, the wheaten-headed hound. . . .

I shall never forget the Thursday when the thing happened. I retired to my room at about six o'clock, fortified with a pony of porter and two threepenny cigars, and manfully addressed myself to the achievement of Chapter Five. McDaid, who for a whole week had been living precariously by selling kittens to foolish old ladies and who could be said to be existing on the immoral earnings of his cat, was required to rob a poor-box in a church. But no! Plot or no plot, it was not to be.

"Sorry, old chap," he said, "but I absolutely can't do it."

†Who is Carruthers McDaid, you ask?

"What's this, Mac," said I, "getting squeamish in your old age?"

"Not squeamish exactly," he replied, "but I bar poor-boxes. Dammit, you can't call me squeamish. Think of that bedroom business in Chapter Two, you old dog."

"Not another word," said I sternly, "you remember that new shaving brush you bought?"

"Yes."

"Very well, you burst the poor-box or it's anthrax in two days."

"But, I say, old chap, that's a bit thick."

"You think so? Well, I'm old-fashioned enough to believe that your opinions don't matter."

We left it at that. Each of us firm, outwardly polite, perhaps, but determined to yield not one tittle of our inalienable rights. It was only afterwards that the whole thing came out. Knowing that he was a dyed-in-the-wool atheist, I had sent him to a revivalist prayer-meeting, purely for the purpose of scoffing and showing the reader the blackness of his soul. It appears that he remained to pray. Two days afterwards I caught him sneaking out to Gardiner Street at seven in the morning. Furthermore, a contribution to the funds of a well-known charity, a matter of four-and-sixpence in the name of Miles Caritatis was not, I understand, unconnected with our proselyte. A character ratting on his creator and exchanging the pre-destined hangman's rope for a halo is something new. It is, however, only one factor in my impending dissolution. Shaun Svoolish, my hero, the composition of whose heroics have cost me many a sleepless day, has formed an alliance with a slavey in Griffith Avenue; and Shiela, his "steady," an exquisite creature I produced for the sole purpose of loving him and becoming his wife, is apparently to be given the air. You see? My carefully thought-out plot is turned inside out and goodness knows where this individualist flummery is going to end. Imagine sitting down to finish a chapter and running bang into an unexplained slavey at the turn of a page! I reproached Shaun, of course.

"Frankly, Shaun," I said, "I don't like it."

"I'm sorry," he said. "My brains, my brawn, my hands, my body are willing to work for you, but the heart! Who shall say yea or nay to the timeless passions of a man's heart? Have you ever been in love? Have you ever—?"

"What about Shiela, you shameless rotter? I gave her dimples, blue eyes, blonde hair and a beautiful soul. The last time she met you, I rigged her out in a blue swagger outfit, brand new. You now throw the whole lot back in my face. . . . Call it cricket if you like, Shaun, but don't expect me to agree."

"I may be a prig," he replied, "but I know what I like. Why can't I marry Bridie and have a shot at the Civil Service?"

"Railway accidents are fortunately rare," I said finally, "but when they happen they are horrible. Think it over."

"You wouldn't dare!"

"O, wouldn't I? Maybe you'd like a new shaving brush as well."

And that was that.

Treason is equally widespread among the minor characters. I have been confronted with a Burmese shanachy, two corner-boys, a barmaid, and five bus-drivers, none of whom could give a satisfactory explanation of their existence or a plausible account of their movements. They are evidently "friends" of my characters. The only character to yield me undivided and steadfast allegiance is a drunken hedonist who is destined to be killed with kindness in Chapter Twelve. *And he knows it!* Not that he is any way lacking in cheek, of course. He started nagging me one evening.

"I say, about the dust-jacket—"

"Yes?"

"No damn vulgarity, mind. Something subtle, refined. If the thing was garish or cheap, I'd die of shame."

"Felix," I snapped, "mind your own business."

Just one long round of annoyance and petty persecution. What is troubling me just at the moment, however, is a paper-knife. I introduced it in an early scene to give Father Hennessy something to fiddle with on a parochial call. It is now in the hands of McDaid. It has a dull steel blade, and there is evidently something going on. The book is seething with conspiracy and there have been at least two whispered consultations between all the characters, including two who have not yet been officially created. Posterity taking a hand in the destiny of its ancestors, if you know what I mean. It is too bad. The only objector, I understand, has been Captain Fowler, the drunken hedonist, who insists that there shall be no foul play until

Chapter Twelve has been completed; and he has been over-ruled.

Candidly, reader, I fear my number's up.

* * * * * * *

I sit at my window thinking, remembering, dreaming. Soon I go to my room to write. A cool breeze has sprung up from the west, a clean wind that plays on men at work, on boys at play and on women who seek to police the corridors, live in Stephen's Green and feel the heat of buckshee turf. . . .

It is a strange world, but beautiful. How hard it is, the hour of parting. I cannot call in the Guards, for we authors have our foolish pride. The destiny of Brother Barnabas is sealed, sealed for aye.

I must write!

These, dear reader, are my last words. Keep them and cherish them. Never again can you read my deathless prose, for my day that has been a good day is past.

Remember me and pray for me.

Adieu!

John Duffy's Brother (1940)

by Flann O'Brien

Strictly speaking, this story should not be written or told at all. To write it or to tell it is to spoil it. This is because the man who had the strange experience we are going to talk about never mentioned it to anybody, and the fact that he kept his secret and sealed it up completely in his memory is the whole point of the story. Thus we must admit that handicap at the beginning—that it is absurd for us to tell the story, absurd for anybody to listen to it, and unthinkable that anybody should believe it.

We will, however, do this man one favour. We will refrain from mentioning him by his complete name. This will enable us to tell his secret and permit him to continue looking his friends in the eye. But we can say that his surname is Duffy. There are thousands of these Duffys in the world; even at this moment there is probably a new Duffy making his appearance in some corner of it. We can even go so far as to say that he is John Duffy's brother. We do not break faith in saying so, because if there are only one hundred John Duffys in existence, and even if each one of them could be met and questioned, no embarrassing enlightenments would be forthcoming. That is because the John Duffy in question never left his house, never left his bed, never talked to anybody in his life, and was never seen by more than one man. That man's name was Gumley. Gumley was a doctor. He was present when John Duffy was born and also when he died, one hour later.

John Duffy's brother lived alone in a small house on an eminence in Inchicore. When dressing in the morning he could gaze across the broad valley of the Liffey to the slopes of the Phoenix Park, peacefully. Usually the river was indiscernible but on a sunny morning it could be seen lying like a long glistening spear in the valley's palm. Like a respectable married man, it seemed to be hurrying into Dublin as if to work.

Sometimes recollecting that his clock was fast, John Duffy's brother would spend an idle moment with his father's spyglass, ranging the valley with an eagle eye. The village of Chapelizod was to the left and invisible in the depth but each morning the inhabitants would erect, as if for Mr. Duffy's benefit, a lazy plume of smoke to show exactly where they were.

Mr. Duffy's glass usually came to rest on the figure of a man hurrying across the uplands of the Park and disappearing from view in the direction of the Magazine Fort. A small white terrier bounced along ahead of him but could be seen occasionally sprinting to overtake him after dallying behind for a time on private business.

The man carried in the crook of his arm an instrument which Mr. Duffy at first took to be a shotgun or patent repeating rifle, but one morning the man held it by the butt and smote the barrels smartly on the ground as he walked, and it was then evident to Mr. Duffy—he felt some disappointment—that the article was a walking-stick.

It happened that this man's name was Martin Smullen. He was a retired stationary-engine driver and lived quietly with a delicate sister at Number Four Cannon Row, Parkgate. Mr. Duffy did not know his name and was destined never to meet him or have the privilege of his acquaintance, but it may be worth mentioning that they once stood side by side at the counter of a public house in Little Easter Street, mutually unrecognised, each to the other a black stranger. Mr. Smullen's call was whiskey, Mr. Duffy's stout.

Mr. Smullen's sister's name was not Smullen but Goggins, relict of the late Paul Goggins, wholesale clothier. Mr. Duffy had never even heard of her. She had a cousin by the name of Leo Corr who was not unknown to the police. He was sent up in 1924 for a stretch of hard labour in connection with the manufacture of spurious currency. Mrs. Goggins had never met him, but heard that he had emigrated to Labrador on his release.

About the spyglass. A curious history attaches to its owner, also a Duffy, late of the Mercantile Marine. Although unprovided with the benefits of a University education—indeed, he had gone to sea at the age of sixteen as a result of an incident arising out of an imperfect understanding of the sexual relation—he was of a scholarly turn of mind and would often spend the afternoons of his sea-leave alone in his dining-room thumbing a book of Homer with delight or annotating with erudite sneers the inferior Latin of the Angelic Doctor. On the fourth day of July, 1927, at four o'clock, he took leave of his senses in the dining-room. Four men arrived in a closed van at eight o'clock that evening to remove him from mortal ken to a place where he would be restrained for his own good.

It could be argued that much of the foregoing has little real bearing on the story of John Duffy's brother, but modern writing, it is hoped, has passed the stage when simple events are stated in the void without any clue as to the psychological and hereditary forces working in the background to produce them. Having said so much, however, it is now permissible to set down briefly the nature of the adventure of John Duffy's brother.

He arose one morning—on the 9th of March, 1932—dressed, and cooked his frugal breakfast. Immediately afterwards, he became possessed of the strange idea that he was a train. No explanation of this can be attempted. Small boys sometimes like to pretend that they are trains, and there are fat women in the world who are not, in the distance, without some resemblance to trains. But John Duffy's brother was certain that he *was* a train—long, thunderous, and immense, with white steam escaping noisily from his feet and deep-throated bellows coming rhythmically from where his funnel was.

Moreover, he was certain that he was a particular train, the 9.20 into Dublin. His station was the bedroom. He stood absolutely still for twenty minutes, knowing that a good train is equally punctual in departure as in arrival. He glanced often at his watch to make sure that the hour should not go by unnoticed. His watch bore the words "Shockproof" and "Railway Timekeeper."

Precisely at 9.20 he emitted a piercing whistle, shook the great mass of his metal ponderously into motion, and steamed away heavily into town. The train arrived dead on time at its destination, which was the office of Messrs. Polter and Polter, Solicitors, Commissioners for Oaths. For obvious reasons, the name of this firm is fictitious. In the office were two men, old Mr. Cranberry and young Mr. Hodge. Both were clerks and both took their orders from John Duffy's brother. Of course, both names are imaginary.

"Good Morning, Mr. Duffy," said Mr. Cranberry. He was old and polite, grown yellow in the firm's service.

Mr. Duffy looked at him in surprise. "Can you not see I am a train?" he said. "Why do you call me Mr. Duffy?"

Mr. Cranberry gave a laugh and winked at Mr. Hodge who sat

young, neat and good-looking, behind his typewriter.

"Alright, Mr. Train," he said. "That's a cold morning, sir. Hard to get up steam these cold mornings, sir."

"It is not easy," said Mr. Duffy. He shunted expertly to his chair and waited patiently before he sat down while the company's servants adroitly uncoupled him. Mr. Hodge was sniggering behind his roller.

"Any cheap excursions, sir?" he asked.

"No," Mr. Duffy replied. "There are season tickets, of course."

"Third class and first class, I suppose, sir?"

"No," said Mr. Duffy. "In deference to the views of Herr Marx, all class distinctions in the passenger rolling-stock have been abolished."

"I see," said Mr. Cranberry.

"That's communism," said Mr. Hodge.

"He means," said Mr. Cranberry, "that it is now first-class only."

"How many wheels has your engine?" asked Mr. Hodge. "Three big ones?"

"I am not a goods train," said Mr. Duffy acidly. "The wheel formation of a passenger engine is four-four-two—two large driving wheels on each side, coupled, of course, with a four-wheel bogey in front and two small wheels at the cab. Why do you ask?"

"The platform's in the way," Mr. Cranberry said. "He can't see it."

"Oh, quite," said Mr. Duffy. "I forgot."

"I suppose you use a lot of coal?" Mr. Hodge said.

"About half-a-ton per thirty miles," said Mr. Duffy slowly, mentally checking the consumption of that morning. "I need scarcely say that frequent stopping and starting at suburban stations takes a lot out of me."

"I'm sure it does," said Mr. Hodge, with sympathy.

They talked like that for half an hour until the elderly Mr. Polter arrived and passed gravely into his back office. When that happened, conversation was at an end. Little was heard until lunch-time except the scratch of pens and the fitful clicking of the typewriter.

John Duffy's brother always left the office at one thirty and went home to his lunch. Consequently he started getting steam up at twelve forty five so that there should be no delay at the hour of departure. When the "Railway Timekeeper" said that it was one thirty, he let out another shrill whistle and steamed slowly out of the office without a word or a look at his colleagues. He arrived home dead on time.

We now approach the really important part of the plot, the incident which gives the whole story its significance. In the middle of his lunch John Duffy's brother felt something important, something queer, momentous, and magical taking place inside his brain, an immense tension relaxing, clean light flooding a place which had been dark. He dropped his knife and fork and sat there for a time wild-eyed, a filling of potatoes unattended in his mouth. Then he swallowed, rose weakly from the table and walked to the window, wiping away the perspiration which had started out on his brow.

He gazed out into the day, no longer a train, but a badly frightened man. Inch by inch he went back over his morning. So far as he could recall he had killed no one, shouted no bad language, broken no windows. He had only talked to Cranberry and Hodge. Down in the roadway there was no dark van arriving with uniformed men infesting it. He sat down again desolately beside the unfinished meal.

John Duffy's brother was a man of some courage. When he got back to the office he had some whiskey in his stomach and it was later in the evening than it should be. Hodge and Cranberry seemed preoccupied with their letters. He hung up his hat casually and said:

"I'm afraid the train is a bit late getting back."

From below his downcast brows he looked very sharply at Cranberry's face. He thought he saw the shadow of a smile flit absently on the old man's placid features as they continued poring down on a paper. The smile seemed to mean that a morning's joke was not good enough for the same evening. Hodge rose suddenly in his corner and passed silently into Mr. Polter's office with his letters. John Duffy's brother sighed and sat down wearily at his desk.

When he left the office that night, his heart was lighter and he thought he had a good excuse for buying more liquor. Nobody knew his secret but himself and nobody else would ever know.

It was a complete cure. Never once did the strange malady return. But to this day John Duffy's brother starts at the rumble of a train in the Liffey tunnel and stands rooted to the road when he comes suddenly on a level-crossing—silent, so to speak, upon a peak in Darien.

When I Met William of Orange (1942)

Footnote to the Battle of the Boyne

by Flann O'Brien

"When I Would Wish to Have Lived, and Why"
No. 17 *of a Series.*

> *When the Editor asked me to write about the period in Irish history in which I would prefer to have lived, I had many doubts and misgivings. There seemed to be an endless selection of periods from which to choose, each of them offering a better prospect than the dreary and dangerous present. I went to bed with the problem and had a curious dream which I reproduce below. It seems that had I lived in the days of King William and King James, I might at least have made myself useful.*
>
> —Flann O'Brien[1]

"It was a bad business all right," said William, edging over to me. "By the way, has he got the pipes on again?"

"He has," I muttered.

"Well now, wouldn't you think it's warm enough without the pipes? He's a terrible man, there's no doubt about it. Tell me now," he added confidentially, "how did you get into it at all? Were you walked into it?"

"Not at all. I blame nobody but myself."

William coughed and tried to wave the swirling black smoke away from his red eyes.

"Those pipes," he said, "are very bad for anybody with a weak chest. They dry up the air, you know. Where were we? Oh, yes, the Battle of the Boyne. Tell me about it. How did *you* get mixed up in it? You don't look like a fighting man, if you'll pardon the remark."

"Indeed?"

"Of course, an Irish cripple could best ten able-bodied foreign-

[1] Editors' Note: This is the headnote to the original story printed in the *Irish Digest* (April 1942), p. 20.

ers—I know that," he said hastily, "or at least so they say in America. But what happened to you?"

"Nothing," I said sulkily. "I just couldn't mind my own business."

"Tell me about it. I like you, you know. I'm sure you have a background."

"I used to live beside the Boyne . . ." I began.

"A nice river," he remarked, "and nice country. As nice a piece of landscape as was ever seen in Holland."

"I used to live beside the Boyne, half naked in a wooden hut. We were real Irish and very poor, you know. The only thing we had was our religion. We were very strict R.Cs. We were more Roman than the Romans themselves."

"On the lines of *Hiberniores*—"

"We spoke Irish at the time, but my father was a native speaker of English, and at a time, if I may say so, when it was neither popular nor profitable. *Caith uait an Ghaedhilg*, I remember him saying, *tá na bodaigh gallda ag teacht agus ní bheidh aon mheas aca uirthi.*'"[2]

"It's a great thing now in the schools—the Irish," William remarked.

"One day I was out fishing for the dinner. I don't know whether you ever tasted a Boyne salmon. . . ."

William made a clicking sound, ran his flat palm in a circle round his stomach and put a look of rapture on his blackened face.

"I remember once in England I lost as nice a piece of tackle as you ever—"

"I kept changing the bait. After a while I began to feel that there was something in the air. Occasionally I heard the gallop of big companies of horsemen in the distance. Now and again I would hear men calling and a noise like the rumble of heavy carts on stony ground. It was all far away but there seemed to be a lot of people moving about the place. I couldn't understand it. It wasn't a fair day or anything."

"I wasn't very far away from you just then," William said, smiling.

"Then a couple of guns went off—accidentally, I suppose. The bang

[2] "Cast the Gaelic away from you . . . those foreign clowns are coming, and they'll have no respect for it." [Trans. Jack Fennell.]

gave me a terrible start. I nearly lept into the water. And whether the fish got a fright, too, I don't know, but a big fellow suddenly swallied hook, sinker, and all. It took me ten minutes to get him out. He weighed twelve pounds and he was that length—look."

I held out my charred hands.

"Now, now," said William chidingly.

"On my solemn oath."

"All right," said William. "No offence. Go on."

"With my fish caught and queer noises in the air, I needn't tell you that I thought that the right place to be was home. And home I went."

"Fair enough," said William.

"When I reached the hut I nearly fell out of my standing with surprise. Here at the door by your leave were two foreign-looking blackguards of soldiers with fancy uniforms talking to my poor old mother—or trying to. They hadn't a word of Irish between the pair of them."

"I see."

"What do you think they wanted?"

"Roughly speaking, I could think of about two hundred things that those boys were fond of."

"Buttermilk!"

"*Buttermilk?*"

"Buttermilk."

William smiled knowingly and shook his head.

"I'll tell you something," he said. "My guess is that they had had a big night the night before. They were a pair of Dutch Blue Guards, if I'm not mistaken. Terrible men, drunk night and morning."

"They looked pretty bad all right. I got talking to them. They said there was going to be a big war. They mentioned a lot of foreign names I could not take in properly. Then they started shaking hands and looking very friendly. Do you know why?"

"Search me," William said.

"They saw something in the house that told them we were Catholics. *Be damned but they were Catholics too!* They were. We got very pally, as thick as thieves. They told me about grand big cathedrals across the sea and we drank the Pope's health in buttermilk. I couldn't take my eyes off their uniforms. You never seen the like—gold braid and buckles and whistles on fancy cords and muskets with ornamental work on the breech.

"I asked one would I get a uniform, whistle and all, if I joined up. He said certainly. Your other man then piped up about what he called 'pickings.' You got the pickings in the pockets of dead soldiers. He said the soldiers that died were always on the other side.

"'Listen here, Bonaparte,' says I to myself—by the way, I haven't seen that fellow knocking around here for a while; maybe your man gave him the oven for some breach of discipline—'listen here, Bonaparte,' says I to myself, 'you're wasting your time in this hole. Join the army and see the world.' *Why the hell didn't I mind my own business instead of meddling with foreigners and politics?* Tell me that?"

I turned to William with some heat. He only made a helpless gesture and rolled his red eyes.

"Well, you know the rest. I got not only my fine uniform but the father and the mother of a cannonball in the small of the b—— back. I went into action on the Friday. They tell me I looked a fierce sight when I was found on the Saturday. No head."

William frowned sympathetically, making a tch tch noise.

"And no back or front to speak of either."

"James was a divil," William said. "That lad Sarsfield was handy with guns, too. Oh, a bad business."

"But what makes me laugh is that those priceless Dutch Blue Guards were in the thick of the fight from the first minute and me thinking they were only there for showing off the uniforms. It was the Catholic Blue Guards that won the Battle of the Boyne and not the Protestants."

William sighed sadly and looked pensive.

"You are quite right. I am the greatest dead authority on the Battle of the Boyne, and I know that next to my own leadership the Dutch Guards was what put the Irish on their backs. Of course James did the dirty on them, but I don't think any other king could have stood up to the boys in blue. Do you smell something burning?"

"It's ourselves. And it was only when I was dead that I got the queer land. I had to fill up a form saying which side I was fighting with. When I said proudly the Roman Catholic Blue Guards there was a big laugh. I was told I'd be put with my pals and here I am."

"I remember the lads well," William said reminiscently.

"If I had my time again," I said, "I'd ask for nothing better than to live the time I did live. I'd get the Dutch Guards to fight for James and then things wouldn't be the way they are in Belfast to-day. I'd explain to them that James was fighting for liberty of conscience, the rights of small nations, truth, honour—"

"*Who's using bad language here?*" a horrible voice said behind us. It was The Man of the House himself. He had a smoky lantern swinging from one of his horns, casting a red glow on what he called his face. He always spoke in italics. I muttered some excuse.

"*Never let me hear filthy words like those again,*" he barked, "*or you'll get the oven.*" Then he moved away, leaving a very heavy important silence behind him.

"Yes, that's what I'd do," I said after a while. "If I lived again in those days I'd get the man who won the Battle of the Boyne over on the side of the Irish."

"I think you're right, lad," William said. "I wonder did I ever show you this? It's a little thing I wrote recently myself. Can you think of any way of getting it down to the *Skibbereen Eagle?*"

He took a charred piece of paper out of his gutted suit and handed it to me modestly. It was a little poem.

"Bed to work and work to bed,
That's what makes my eye-lids red,
I'd rather live in Herbert Park
And count my banknotes after dark,
Or live in Stormont at a pinch
Refusing all who want an inch."

We both laughed sulphureously.

"*Maith a' fear,*" I said. [3]

Then we parted, probably for another hundred years, for the crowd is big here and the congestion is increasing year by year.

[3] Trans. "Good man."

I'm Telling You No Lie! (1943)

Some leaves from the author's salad days

by Lir O'Connor

A Character I Could Never Forget.
No. 30 *of a Series.*

> *Looking back across the years of a lifetime as colourful as it has been exciting, I think I shall experience little difficulty in the selection of a suitable subject for this feature. For, I ask you, what more memorable, more breath-taking character could I possibly find to write about than my own inimitable self? True, in a volume of this size I can only hope to give the merest outline of a personality so vital that it might well have been the invention of some master of the romantic novel; but then this will be more than compensated for by the fact that my publishers will not be faced with the costs of the customary libel action which nowadays normally follows on every reference in print to any name, proper or otherwise, that is not, strictly speaking, one's own.*
>
> —Lir O'Connor[1]

I started off in life with somewhat of a handicap. Only those who were born in Ballyjoesullivan will know what I mean. The kindly caress of a mother's hand was denied to me from the beginning, as poor Mum had come to a tragic end some two years before I was born, having been fatally shot through the corsage in a saloon brawl. Someone had spoken lightly of a horse-jobber's name. Poor Dad was worse than useless at this time, having one foot in the grave, and the other, for nine months out of the twelve, confined within the narrow framework of a Thomas splint. I often wonder how I ever managed to survive, but there—let us commence at the beginning.

The ragged storm clouds were veiling the face of the moon on the 3rd of September, 1886. Midnight chimed from the village church,

[1] Editors' Note: This is the headnote to the original story printed in the *Irish Digest* (July 1943), p. 15.

and the sound of the bells had scarcely been whipped away by the fingers of the gale when, high above the soughing of the wind, there was heard the wailing cry of a new-born baby. For that day and hour was I born, much to my uncle's and aunt's embarrassment. It is scarcely necessary to add that I was born with a caul, since practically every writer worth slandering was born with a caul, from Dickens down to Shelly. (I don't mean Percy B. Shelley, but a man named Fonsie Shelly I used to know who did odd pars for the old *Freeman's Journal.*)

Ah! If I had a mind to tell it, the subsequent history of that little caul would fill a good-sized book in itself. I could relate how, tied up with an old boot lace into a compact sphere, it helped me to win by a comfortable margin the senior hardball championships at Ballymun at an age when most boys are playing with their bead frames. Years later, when wintering in Siberia, it occupied the centre of the stage again. Most of my companions had died of cold and starvation. The very last pair of Russian boots had been ravenously devoured by us after having been converted into the savoury borsch that only the Russians can make. Day after day I could see the red-rimmed eyes of the others straying hungrily to the palatable tit-bit that I was using as a droshky rug. Let me cut a long story short by saying that it was only by sleeping with a half-cocked moose gun under my pillow at night that I contrived to stave them off until help finally arrived. To this very day it remains my constant travelling companion, for, stretched out on a light bamboo frame, it constitutes the highly efficient punkah with which one of my "boys" is agitating the sultry atmosphere even as I pen these few words. However, I must not bore you with irrelevant details.

Where was I? Oh! Yes—I had just been born. Well, no sooner did I divest my chubby little face of its lucky charm than I buried my needle-sharp fangs in the arm of the old midwife who presided at my *début.* This pretty display of temperament won for me the sobriquet of "Ballyjoesullivan Tiger Cat," a name which clung to me long after Ballyjoesullivan had become nothing more than an unsavoury memory. Little did I think at the time that those small, white teeth would soon enable me to supplement Dad's meagre earnings as postmaster of that barony, on the site of which a world-famous synthetic rope factory now stands. Like most rural post offices ours was devoid of those little articles of office equipment that make the life of a postmaster tolerable in a hamlet so primitive that the nearest public house was more than 200 yards away. No damp sponge in a delph container decorated the counter. I think it is no exaggeration to say that I was almost a fully-grown man before I could distinguish without hesitation between an all-steel filing cabinet and a patent clip-fastener. The official pen was so rusty that neighbouring farmers used to purchase the sediment in the ink-well for use as a top dressing of iron for their vast onion plantations.

It goes, therefore, without saying, that we had no dentotype stamp perforator. The result was that, night after night, poor Dad and I used to sit up, he steaming open the villagers' letters with his bronchitis kettle, and I with my tiny incisors making the necessary punctures in the broad sheets of unfinished stamps that used to come down to us by canal boat from the G.P.O. in Dublin. Later on, when his sight began to fail, I took over the task of making digests of such letters as might prove remunerative when the parties concerned would come into the office to lodge something in their savings account. Life was no bed of roses for Dad and me in those days, and it was only by making intelligent use of their infirmity, when blind pensioners came to draw their allowance, that we were able to carry on until the Great War put the business on its feet.

Like many healthy striplings of my age, when I was fifteen I ran away to sea, but having greater intellectual powers than most lads in their 'teens, I soon saw the folly of my ways, and ran back again. There I remained until Dad passed on, leaving to me the post office in his will. The old place fetched a fancy price from the village gombeen man about whom I knew a few things he appeared to want to keep dark. Or maybe he saw possibilities for himself in the little game of "postman's knock" as played by Dad and me. Who knows? At all events it was with a light heart and with pockets stuffed with blood money and postal orders that I turned my back on my native village never to return.

All my life I had wanted to be a writer, so when a magazine advertisement caught my eye explaining how you can earn £10 a week in your spare time writing stories, I immediately sent off one of my postal orders and commenced the requisite correspondence course. This was my first step towards success. Of course, at first, publishing firms declined to pay me the £10 a week which I demanded for my work. But far from discouraging me, this had precisely the opposite effect. Course after course of tuition did I take with different schools, even going so far as to take out a two-term course in personality-development in case I should ever come up against some headstrong publisher face to face. I was very nearly down to my last money order when I paused to ask myself who was making £10 a week out of all this. As the answer came to me in a flash, I rushed off to rent a small room, gave myself a few honorary university degrees, and, on the same day, inaugurated the Royal Literary Correspondence College, the stately buildings of which can be seen in any large city to-day, eloquent testimony to the success which has crowned my youthful literary efforts.

Coming to think of it, I suppose I *have* been fairly successful. Money no longer means very much to me. The self-conferred degrees of my earlier days have been replaced by doctorates and diplomas conferred by the most august universities and academies in Europe. I have been forced to give up living in exclusive hotels because of the hordes of playwrights, authors, and professors of literature who made my life unbearable with their endless toadying, touching of hats and touting for tutorships. I take very little part in the world-wide activities of the College nowadays, beyond an indulgent glance at the balance-sheet which my fellow-directors fake up for me once a year. My home is just wherever I care to drop the anchor of my favourite yacht. Where am I now, you will probably want to know? Well, in case there are any job-cadging littérateurs among my readers, the most I care to say is that I am, at the moment, about 4,000 miles from my native soil. From the shady verandah where I am sitting with a long, cool drink in my hand I can see the natives unloading the brightly coloured bales of cotton from the fussy little steamer, which every three months ties up to the rotten waterlogged old timbers of the jetty.

Just beside the toe of my boot is one of the vivid green, white, and yellow grass lizards which the Krooboys make into tasteful handbags for their womenfolk. I do not raise my foot to crush it. Why, I wonder? Perhaps I am just too lazy to do so. Or perhaps it is because—and here, I believe, we are getting nearer to the truth—the colours of the creature have awakened in me a feeling that I had thought was long since dead. For, whenever I hear a few bars from an old Irish song or have a few glasses of an old Irish whiskey my thoughts go out across oceans and continents to the land where I was born. Through the swirling mists I can picture a little thatched, whitewashed crubeen on the side of a hill. Leaning over the half-door, a leather-faced bonnav-dealer[2] puffs away at his blackened old cruiskeen lawn as he gazes down thoughtfully into the valley. Through the smoky twilight within I see his aged help-meet, or colleen bawn, crouching over the turf fire stirring away at her three-legged poteen of carrageen, pausing now and then to gather an odd sad air from her harpeen. With a heart too full for words I reflect that this is *my* country, and that these people are my own kith and kin, and something like a prayer escapes me as I sob: "Oh! Thank heaven to be away from it all!"

[2] An Anglicization of the Gaelic word "banbh," meaning "piglet."

Drink and Time in Dublin

by Myles na gCopaleen

A Recorded Statement

—Did you go to that picture *The Lost Weekend*?

—*I did.*

—I never seen such tripe.

—*What was wrong with it?*

—O it was all right, of course—bits of it was good. Your man in the jigs inside the bed and the bat flying in to kill the mouse, that was *damn* good. I'll tell you another good bit. Hiding the bottles in the jax. And there was no monkey business about that because I tried it since meself. It works but you have to use the half-pint bottles. Up the chimbley is another place I thought of and do you know the ledge affair above windows?

—*I do.*

—That's another place but you could get a hell of a fall reaching up there on a ladder or standing on chairs with big books on them. And of course you can always tie the small bottles to the underneath of your mattress.

—*I suppose you can.*

—But what are you to do with the empties if you stop in bed drinking? There's a snag there. I often thought they should have malt in lemonade syphons.

—*Why didn't you like the rest of* The Lost Weekend*?*

—Sure haven't I been through far worse weekends meself—you know that as well as I do. Sure Lord save us I could tell you yarns. I'd be a rich man if I had a shilling for every morning I was down in the markets at seven o'clock in the slippers with the trousers pulled on over the pyjamas and the overcoat buttoned up to the neck in the middle of the summer. Sure don't be talking man.

—*I suppose the markets are very congested in the mornings?*

—With drunks? I don't know. I never looked round any time I was there.

—*When were you last there?*

—The time the wife went down to Cork last November. I won't

forget that business in a hurry. That was a scatter and a half. Did I never tell you about that? O be God, don't get me on to that affair.

—*Was it the worst ever?*

—It was and it wasn't but I got the fright of me life. I'll tell you a damn good one. You won't believe this but it's a true bill. This is one of the best you ever heard.

—*I'll believe anything you say.*

—In the morning I brought the wife down to Kingsbridge in a taxi. I wasn't thinking of drink at all, hadn't touched it for four months, but when I paid the taxi off at the station instead of going back in it, the wife gave me a look. Said nothing, of course—after the last row I was for keeping off the beer for a year. But somehow she put the thing into me head. This was about nine o'clock, I suppose. I'll give you three guesses where I found meself at ten past nine in *another taxi*?

—*Where?*

—Above in the markets. And there wasn't a more surprised man than meself. Of course in a way it's a good thing to start at it early in the morning because with no food and all the rest of it you're finished at four o'clock and you're home again and stuffed in bed. It's the late nights that's the killer, two and three in the morning, getting poisoned in shebeens and all classes of hooky stuff, wrong change, and a taxi man on the touch. After nights like that it's a strong man that'll be up at the markets in time next morning.

—*What happened after the day you got back at four?*

—Up at the markets next morning *before* they were open. There was another chap there but I didn't look at him. I couldn't tell you what age he was or how bad he was. There was no four o'clock stuff that day. I was around the markets till twelve or so. Then off up town and I have meself shaved be a barber. Then up to a certain hotel and straight into the bar. There's a whole crowd there that I know. What are you going to have and so on. No no, have a large one. So-and-so's getting married on Tuesday. Me other man's wife has had a baby. You know the stuff? Well Lord save us I had a terrible tank of malt in me that day! I had a feed in the middle of it because I remember scalding myself with hot coffee and I never touch the coffee at all only after a feed. Of course I don't remember what happened me but I was in the flat the next morning with the clothes half off. I was supposed to be staying with the brother-in-law, of course, when the wife was away. But sure it's the old dog for the hard road. Drunk or sober I went back to me own place. As a matter of fact I never went near the brother-in-law at all. Be this time I was well into the malt. Out with me again feeling like death on wires and I'm inside in the local curing meself for hours, spilling stuff all over the place with the shake in the hand. Then into the barber's and after that off up again to the hotel for more malt. I'll give you a tip. Always drink in hotels. If you're in there you're in for a feed, or you've just had a feed or you've an appointment there to see a fellow, and you're having a small one to pass the time. It looks very bad being in bars during the daytime. It's a thing to watch, that.

—*What happened then*?

—What do you think happened? What could happen? I get meself into a quiet corner and I start lowering them good-o. I don't know what happened to me, of course. I met a few pals and there is some business about a greyhound out in Cloghran. It was either being bought or being sold and I go along in the taxi and where we were and where we weren't I couldn't tell you. I fall asleep on a chair in some house in town and next thing I wake up perished with the cold and as sick as I ever was in me life. Next thing I know I'm above in the markets. Taxis everywhere of course, no food only the plate of soup in the hotel, and be this time the cheque-book is in and out of the pocket *three or four times a day*, standing drinks all round, kicking up a barney in the lavatory with other drunks, looking for me "rights" when I was refused drink—O, blotto, there's no other word for it. I seen some of the cheques since. *The writing!* A pal carts me home in a taxi. How long this goes on I don't know. I'm all right in the middle of the day but in the mornings I'm nearly too weak to walk and the shakes getting worse every day. Be this time I'm getting frightened of meself. Lookat here, mister-me-man, I say to meself, this'll have to stop. I was afraid the heart might give out, that was the only thing I was afraid of. Then I meet a pal of mine that's a doctor. This is inside the hotel. There's only one man for you, he says, and that's sleep. Will you go home and go to bed if I get you something that'll make you sleep? Certainly, I said. I suppose this was about four or half four. Very well, says he, I'll write you out a prescription. He writes one out on hotel notepaper. I send for a porter. Go across with this, says I, to the nearest chemist shop and get this stuff for me and here's two bob for yourself. Of course I'm at the whiskey all the time. Your man comes back with a box of long-shaped green pills. You'll want to be careful with that stuff, the doctor says, that stuff's very dangerous. If you take one now and take another when you get home, you'll get a very good sleep but don't take any more till to-morrow night because that stuff's very dangerous. So I take one. But I know the doctor doesn't know how bad I am. I didn't tell him the whole story, no damn fear. So out with me to the jax where I take another one. Then back for a drink, still as wide-awake as a lark. You'll have to go home now, the doctor says, we can't have you passing out here, that stuff acts very quickly. Well, I have one more drink and off with me, *in a bus*, mind you, to the flat. I'm very surprised on the bus to find meself so wide-awake, looking out at people and reading the signs on shops. Then I begin to get afraid that the stuff is too weak and that I'll be lying awake for the rest of the evening and all night. To hell with it, I say to meself, we'll chance two more and let that be the end of it. Down went two more in the bus. I get there and into the flat. I'm still wide-awake and nothing will do me only one more pill for luck. I get into bed. I don't remember putting the head on the pillow. I wouldn't go out quicker if you hit me over the head with a crow-bar.

—*You probably took a dangerous over-dose.*

—Next thing I know I'm awake. It's dark. I sit up. There's matches there and I strike one. I look at the watch. The watch is stopped. I get up and look at the clock. Of course the clock is stopped, hasn't been wound for days. I don't know what time it is. I'm a bit upset about this. I turn on the wireless. It takes about a year to heat up and would you believe me I try a dozen stations all over the place and not one of them is telling what the time is. Of course I knew there was no point in trying American stations. I'm very disappointed because I sort of expected a voice to say "It is now seven thirty P.M." or whatever the time was. I turn off the wireless and begin to wonder. I don't know what time it is. *Then*, bedamnit, another thing strikes me. *What day is it?* How long have I been asleep with that dose? Well lookat, I got a hell of a fright when I found I didn't know what day it was. I got one hell of a fright.

—*Was there not an accumulation of milk-bottles or newspapers?*

—There wasn't—all that was stopped because I was supposed to be staying with the brother-in-law. What do I do? On with all the clothes and out to find what time it is and what day it is. The funny thing is I'm not feeling too bad. Off with me down the street. There's lights showing in the houses. That means it's night-time and not early in the morning. Then I see a bus. That means it's not yet half-nine, because they stopped at half-nine that time. Then I see a clock. It's twenty past nine! But I still don't know what day it is and it's too late to buy an evening paper. There's only one thing—into a pub and get a look at one. So I march into the nearest, very quiet and correct and say a bottle of stout please. All the other customers look very sober and I think they are all talking very low. When the man brings me the bottle I say to him I beg your pardon but I had a few bob on a horse today, could you please give me a look at an evening paper? The man looks at me and says what horse was it? It was like a blow in the face to me, that question! I can't answer at all at first and then I stutter something about Hartigan's horses. None of them horses won a race today, the man says, and there was a paper here but it's gone. So I drink up the bottle and march out. It's funny, finding out about the day. You can't stop a man in the street and say have you got the right day please? God knows what would happen if you done that. I know be now that it's no use telling lies about horses, so in with me to another pub, order a bottle and ask the man has he got an evening paper. The missus has it upstairs, he says, there's nothing on it anyway. I now begin to think the best thing is to dial O on the phone, ask for Inquiries and find out that way. I'm on me way to a call-box when I begin to think that's a very bad idea. The girl might say hold on and I'll find out, I hang on there like a mug and next thing the box is surrounded by Guards and ambulances and attendants with ropes. No fear, says I to meself, there's going to be no work on the phone for me! Into another pub. I have to wind up now and no mistake. How long was I knocked out be the drugs? A day? Two days? Was I in bed *for a week*? Suddenly I see a sight that gladdens me heart. Away down at the end of the pub there's an oul' fellow reading an evening paper with a magnifying glass. I take a mouthful of stout, steady meself, and march down to him. Me mind is made up: if he doesn't hand over the paper, I'll kill him. Down I go. Excuse me, says I, snatching the paper away from him and he still keeps looking through the glass with no paper there, I think he was deaf as well as half blind. Then I read the date—I suppose it was the first time the date was the big news on a paper. It says "Thursday, 22nd November, 1945." I never enjoyed a bit of news so much. I hand back the paper and say thanks very much, sir, for the loan of your paper. Then I go back to finish me stout, very happy and pleased with me own cuteness. Another man, I say to meself, would ask people, make a show of himself and maybe get locked up. But not me. I'm smart. Then begob I nearly choked.

—*What was the cause of that?*

—To-day is Thursday, I say to meself. Fair enough. But . . . *what day did I go to bed?* What's the use of knowing to-day's Thursday if I don't know when I went to bed? I still don't know whether I've been asleep for a day or a week! I nearly fell down on the floor. I am back where I started. Only I am feeling weaker and be now I have the wind up in gales. The heart begins to knock so loud that I'm afraid the man behind the counter will hear it and order me out.

—*What did you do?*

—Lookat here, me friend, I say to meself, take it easy. Go back now to the flat and take it easy for a while. This'll all end up all right, everything comes right in the latter end. Worse than this happened many's a man. And back to the flat I go. I collapse down into a chair with the hat still on me head, I sink the face down in me hands, and try to think. I'm like that for maybe five minutes. Then, *suddenly*, I know the answer! Without help from papers or clocks or people, I know how long I am there sleeping under the green pills! How did I know? Think that one out! How would *you* know if you were in the same boat?

(Before continuing, readers may wish to accept the sufferer's challenge.)

—*I am thinking.*

—Don't talk to me about calendars or hunger or anything like that. It's no use—you won't guess. You wouldn't think of it in a million years. Look. My face is in my hands—like this. Suddenly I notice the face is smooth. I'm not badly in need of a shave. That means it *must* be the same day I went to bed on! Maybe the stomach or something woke me up for a second or so. If I'd stopped in bed, I was off asleep again in a minute. But I got up to find the time and that's what ruined me! Now do you get it? Because when I went back to bed that night, I didn't waken till the middle of the next day.

—*You asked me how I would have found out how long I had been there after finding that the day was Thursday. I have no guarantee that a person in your condition would not get up and shave in his sleep. There was a better way.*

—There was no other way.

—*There was. If I were in your place I would have looked at the date on the prescription.*

The Martyr's Crown (1950)

by Brian Nolan

Mr. Toole and Mr. O'Hickey walked down the street together in the morning.

Mr. Toole had a peculiarity. He had the habit, when accompanied by another person, of saluting total strangers; but only if these strangers were of important air and costly raiment. He meant thus to make it known that he had friends in high places, and that he himself, though poor, was a person of quality fallen on evil days through some undisclosed sacrifice made in the interest of immutable principle early in life. Most of the strangers, startled out of their private thoughts, stammered a salutation in return. And Mr. Toole was shrewd. He stopped at that. He said no more to his companion, but by some little private gesture, a chuckle, a shake of the head, a smothered imprecation, he nearly always extracted the one question most melodious to his ear: "*Who was that?*"

Mr. Toole was shabby, and so was Mr. O'Hickey, but Mr. O'Hickey had a neat and careful shabbiness. He was an older and a wiser man, and was well up to Mr. Toole's tricks. Mr. Toole at his best, he thought, was better than a play. And he now knew that Mr. Toole was appraising the street with beady eye.

"Gorawars!" Mr. Toole said suddenly.

We are off, Mr. O'Hickey thought.

"Do you see this hop-off-my-thumb with the stick and the hat?" Mr. Toole said.

Mr. O'Hickey did. A young man of surpassing elegance was approaching; tall, fair, darkly dressed; even at fifty yards his hauteur seemed to chill Mr. O'Hickey's part of the street.

"Ten to one he cuts me dead," Mr. Toole said. "This is one of the most extraordinary pieces of work in the whole world."

Mr. O'Hickey braced himself for a more than ordinary impact. The adversaries neared each other.

"*How are we at all, Sean a chara?*" Mr. Toole called out.

The young man's control was superb. There was no glare, no glance of scorn, no sign at all. He was gone, but had left in his wake so complete an impression of his contempt that even Mr. Toole paled momentarily. The experience frightened Mr. O'Hickey.

"Who . . . who was *that*?" he asked at last.

"I knew the mother well," Mr. Toole said musingly. "The woman was a saint." Then he was silent.

Mr. O'Hickey thought: there is nothing for it but bribery—again. He led the way into a public house and ordered two bottles of stout.

"As you know," Mr. Toole began, "I was Bart Conlon's right-hand man. We were through 'twenty and 'twenty-one together. Bart, of course, went the other way in 'twenty-two."

Mr. O'Hickey nodded and said nothing. He knew that Mr. Toole had never rendered military service to his country.

"In any case," Mr. Toole continued, "there was a certain day early in 'twenty-one and orders come through that there was to be a raid on the Sinn Féin office above in Harcourt Street. There happened to be a certain gawskogue of a cattle-jobber from the County Meath had an office on the other side of the street. And he was well in with a certain character be the name of Mick Collins. I think you get me drift?"

"I do," Mr. O'Hickey said.

"There was six of us," Mr. Toole said, "with meself and Bart Conlon in charge. Me man the cattle-jobber gets an urgent call to be out of his office accidentally on purpose at four o'clock, and at half-four the six of us is parked inside there with two machine-guns, the rifles, and a class of a home-made bomb that Bart used to make in his own kitchen. The military arrived in two lurries on the other side of the street at five o'clock. That was the hour in the orders that come. I believe that man Mick Collins had lads working for him over in the War Office across in London. He was a great stickler for the British being punctual on the dot."

"He was a wonderful organiser," Mr. O'Hickey said.

"Well, we stood with our backs to the far wall and let them have it through the open window and them getting down offa the lurries. Sacred godfathers! I never seen such murder in me life. Your men didn't know where it was coming from, and a lot of them wasn't worried very much when it was all over, because there was no heads left on some of them. Bart then gives the order for retreat down the back stairs; in no time we're in the lane, and five minutes more the six of us upstairs in Martin Fulham's pub in Camden Street. Poor Martin is dead since."

"I knew that man well," Mr. O'Hickey remarked.

"Certainly you knew him well," Mr. Toole said, warmly. "The six of us was marked men, of course. In any case, fresh orders come at six o'clock. All hands was to proceed in military formation, singly, be different routes to the house of a great skin in the Cumann na mBan, a widow be the name of Clougherty that lived on the south side. We were all to lie low, do you understand, till there was fresh orders to come out and fight again. Sacred wars, they were very rough days them days; will I ever forget Mrs. Clougherty! She was certainly a marvellous figure of a woman. I never seen a woman like her to bake bread."

Mr. O'Hickey looked up.

"Was she," he said, "was she . . . all right?"

"She was certainly nothing of the sort," Mr. Toole said loudly and sharply. "By God, we were all thinking of other things in them days. Here was this unfortunate woman in a three-storey house on her own, with some quare fellow in the middle flat, herself on the ground floor, and six blood-thirsty pultogues hiding above on the top floor, every manjack ready to shoot his way out if there was trouble. We got feeds there I never seen before or since, and the *Independent* every morning. Outrage in Harcourt Street. The armed men then decamped and made good their escape. I'm damn bloody sure we made good our escape. There was one snag. We couldn't budge out. No exercise at all—and that means only one thing. . . ."

"Constipation?" Mr. O'Hickey suggested.

"The very man," said Mr. Toole.

Mr. O'Hickey shook his head.

"We were there a week. Smoking and playing cards, but when nine o'clock struck, Mrs. Clougherty come up and, Protestant, Catholic, or Jewman, all hands had to go down on the knees. A very good . . . strict . . . woman, if you understand me, a true daughter of Ireland. And now I'll tell you a damn good one. About five o'clock one evening I heard a noise below and peeped out of the window. Sanctified and holy godfathers!"

"What was it—the noise?" Mr. O'Hickey asked.

"What do you think, only two lurries packed with military, with my nabs of an officer hopping out and running up the steps to hammer at the door, and all the Tommies sitting back with their guns at the ready. Trapped! That's a nice word—*trapped!* If there was ever rats in a cage, it was me unfortunate brave men from the battle of Harcourt Street. God!"

"They had you at what we call a disadvantage," Mr. O'Hickey conceded.

"She was in the room herself with the teapot. She had a big silver satteen blouse on her; I can see it yet. She turned on us and gave us all one look that said: *Shut up, ye nervous lousers.* Then she foostered about a bit at the glass and walks out of the room with bang-bang-bang to shake the house going on downstairs. And I seen a thing. . . ."

"What?" asked Mr. O'Hickey.

"She was a fine—now you'll understand me, Mr. O'Hickey," Mr. Toole said carefully; "I seen her fingers on the buttons of the satteen, if you follow me, and she leaving the room."

Mr. O'Hickey, discreet, nodded thoughtfully.

"I listened at the stairs. Jakers I never got such a drop in me life. She clatters down and flings open the halldoor. This young pup is outside, and asks—awsks—in the law-de-daw voice, 'Is there any men in this house?' The answer took me to the fair altogether. She puts on the guttiest voice I ever heard outside Moore Street and says, 'Sairtintly not at this hour of the night; I wish to God there was. Sure, how could the poor unfortunate women get on without them, officer?' Well lookat. I nearly fell down the stairs on top of the two of them. The next thing I hear is, 'Madam this and madam that' and 'Sorry to disturb and I beg your pardon,' 'I trust this and I trust that,' and then the whispering starts, and at the wind-up the halldoor is closed and into the room off the hall with the pair of them. This young bucko out of the Borderers in a room off the hall with a headquarters captain of the Cumann na mBan! *Give us two more stouts there, Mick!*"

"That is a very queer one, as the man said," Mr. O'Hickey said.

"I went back to the room and sat down. Bart had his gun out, and we were all looking at one another. After ten minutes we heard another noise."

Mr. Toole poured out his stout with unnecessary care.

"It was the noise of the lurries driving away," he said at last. "She'd saved our lives, and when she come up a while later she said, 'We'll go to bed a bit earlier to-night, boys; kneel down all.' That was Mrs. Clougherty the saint."

Mr. O'Hickey, also careful, was working at his own bottle, his wise head bent at the task.

* * * * * *

"What I meant to ask you was this," Mr. O'Hickey said, "that's an extraordinary affair altogether, but what has that to do with that stuck-up young man we met in the street, the lad with all the airs?"

"Do you not see it, man?" Mr. Toole said in surprise. "For seven hundred years, thousands—no, I'll make it millions—of Irish men and women have died for Ireland. We never rared jibbers; they were glad to do it, and will again. But that young man was *born* for Ireland. There was never anybody else like him. Why wouldn't he be proud?"

"The Lord save us!" Mr. O'Hickey cried.

"A saint I called her," Mr. Toole said, hotly. "What am I talking about—she's a martyr and wears the martyr's crown to-day!"

Donabate (1952)

by Myles na gCopaleen

It may seem an odd thing to say that, not so long ago, it was a common thing to see the late Sir Sefton Fleetwood-Crawshaye, O.B.E., very drunk in a rather low Dublin public house—and consorting with questionable fellows. And yet he was the perfect gentleman.

Sir Sefton was an Englishman who had spent an industrious and frugal lifetime looking after British railway stations in the capacity of architect. With his pension and savings, he was well-to-do on retirement but, entertaining great fear of his native country's Socialist Chancellor, hastily settled down in Dublin. Here—a man to whom in the past a small sherry seemed excess—he was induced by some demon to drink a glass of Irish whiskey. It was the glass of doom.

The velocity of his disintegration was startling. He began to drink whiskey all day long—longer, indeed, than the licensing day, for he would rise at seven in the morning to visit the privileged taverns at the markets near the Four Courts.

At about two one day I saw him in a pub with three chaps I knew. I joined the group. Sir Sefton was truly very drunk and had trouble in plucking the particular star he wanted from the constellation of small ones that was arranged on the counter in front of him. Still, he had them all finished when the half-two closing was called. He ordered one of the chaps to call a taxi.

"We will all go to Amiens Street Station," he muttered, "for the holy hour."

I could not dissuade him. We went in the taxi. In the station bar, I ordered five small whiskeys.

"Are ye travellers?" the girl asked.

"We are," I said. I noticed that Sir Sefton was appraising the station's face with his old practised eye.

"I can't serve ye if ye haven't tickets," the girl said.

"Where are we supposed to be from?" I asked.

"Donabate."

Donabate! What a place to must be from, a rolling slobland pocked with cheap bungalows and shacks! I turned to go for the tickets, but Sir Sefton had heard. He held up a flat hand.

"Under no circumstances," he said. "Leave this to me."

He left the bar, heading for the ticket office, using that fast turn of speed which drinkers know to be the only hope of avoiding wild staggers. He returned and pressed five cardboards in my hand. I showed them to the girl and we got our drinks.

I lost sight of Sir Sefton for some weeks, but I was told that he was making a practice of these visits to Amiens Street at half-two, always buying a ticket to Donabate. Being near the station one day during the hour, I remembered this; I went in, bought a ticket to Donabate, and entered the bar. Yes, Sir Sefton Fleetwood-Crawshaye was there. He saluted me.

"Donabate?" he asked.

"Donabate," I said.

He nodded in a musing sort of way, and quietly attacked his drink.

"Do you know," he said after a pause, "I like this country. I should like to give some small service. I am still an architect, I hope. I understand lay-out. Donabate is very much in need of a survey—for that matter so is every town in Ireland. You will admit the main street could be improved. We need new churches, too, everywhere. Immense improvements need not be costly given skilled planning. . . ."

He trailed off into a meditation, reviving to mention the vital importance of squares, otherwise how can one hold huge public meetings? I did not find this amusing. It saddened me.

Each time I met him thereafter, his poor brain had further softened. Overcrowding in Donabate must be ended by the simple expedient of erecting great blocks of flats. The American steel-and-concrete technique would be admirable in such a setting. A race-course would bring much-needed revenue to the town, and were there not great expanses of sand nearby, ideal for gallops? But one must not overlook the necessity for a proper car park, with restaurants, cinemas, and so forth.

On another occasion he discussed, though rather tentatively, the founding of a university at Donabate.

"But first," was ever his final cry, "the survey! The survey first!"

He meant it, too. He was determined some day to go to Donabate to do the survey.

One day, as was deposed at the inquest, he entered the bar, showed his ticket and had a drink. He was carrying the reel of tape surveyors use. He kept looking at the clock and suddenly made a wild exit from the bar, tried to enter a train which was just moving off, fell between the train and the platform and was instantly killed.

I have said he was the perfect gentleman, incapable of a mean act. A month after his death, I put on a raincoat I had not worn for a long time. In the pocket were the five tickets Sir Sefton Fleetwood-Crawshaye insisted on buying the first day we went to the station. Pathetic but noble tokens! They were First Class!

Two in One (1954)

by Myles na Gopaleen

The story I have to tell is a strange one, perhaps unbelievable. I will try to set it down as simply as I can. I do not expect to be disturbed in my literary labours, for I am writing this in the condemned cell.

Let us say my name is Murphy. The unusual occurrence which led me here concerns my relations with another man whom we shall call Kelly. Both of us were taxidermists.

I will not attempt a treatise on what a taxidermist is. The word is ugly and inadequate. Certainly it does not convey to the layman that such an operator must combine the qualities of zoologist, naturalist, chemist, sculptor, artist, and carpenter. Who would blame such a person for showing some temperament now and again, as I did?

It is necessary, however, to say a brief word about this science. First, there is no such thing in modern practice as "stuffing" an animal. There is a record of stuffed gorillas having been in Carthage in the 5th century, and it is a fact that an Austrian prince, Siegmund Herberstein, had stuffed bison in the great hall of his castle in the 16th century—it was then the practice to draw the entrails of animals and to substitute spices and various preservative substances. There is a variety of methods in use to-day but, except in particular cases—snakes, for example, where preserving the translucency of the skin is a problem calling for special measures—the basis of all modern methods is simply this: you skin the animal very carefully according to a certain pattern, and you encase the skinless body in plaster of Paris. You bisect the plaster when cast providing yourself with two complementary moulds from which you can make a casting of the animal's body—there are several substances, all very light, from which such castings can be made. The next step, calling for infinite skill and patience, is to mount the skin on the casting of the body. That is all I need explain here, I think.

Kelly carried on a taxidermy business and I was his assistant. He was the boss—a swinish, overbearing mean boss, a bully, a sadist. He hated me, but enjoyed his hatred too much to sack me. He knew I had a real interest in the work, and a desire to broaden my experience. For that reason, he threw me all the common-place jobs that came in. If some old lady sent her favourite terrier to be done, that was me; foxes and cats and Shetland ponies and white rabbits—they were all strictly *my* department. I could do a perfect job on such animals in my sleep, and got to hate them. But if a crocodile came in, or a Great Borneo spider, or (as once happened) a giraffe—Kelly kept them all for himself. In the meantime he would treat my own painstaking work with sourness and sneers and complaints.

One day the atmosphere in the workshop had been even fouler than usual, with Kelly in a filthier temper than usual. I had spent the forenoon finishing a cat, and at about lunch-time put it on the shelf where he left completed orders.

I could nearly *hear* him glaring at it. Where was the tail? I told him there was no tail, that it was a Manx cat. How did I know it was a Manx cat, how did I know it was not an ordinary cat which had lost its tail in a motor accident or something? I got so mad that I permitted myself a disquisition on cats in general, mentioning the distinctions as between *Felis manul*, *Felis silvestris*, and *Felis lybica*, and on the unique structure of the Manx cat. His reply to that? He called me a slob. That was the sort of life *I* was having.

On this occasion something within me snapped. I was sure I could hear the snap. I had moved up to where he was to answer his last insult. The loathsome creature had his back to me, bending down to put on his bicycle clips. Just to my hand on the bench was one of the long, flat, steel instruments we use for certain operations with plaster. I picked it up and hit him a blow with it on the back of the head. He gave a cry and slumped forward. I hit him again. I rained blow after blow on him. Then I threw the tool away. I was upset. I went out into the yard and looked around. I remembered he had a weak heart. Was he dead? I remember adjusting the position of a barrel we had in the yard to catch rainwater, the only sort of water suitable for some of the mixtures we used. I found I was in a cold sweat but strangely calm. I went back into the workshop.

Kelly was just as I had left him. I could find no pulse. I rolled him over on his back and examined his eyes, for I have seen more lifeless eyes in my day than most people. Yes, there was no doubt: Kelly was dead. I had killed him. I was a murderer. I put on my coat and hat and left the place. I walked the streets for a while, trying to avoid panic, trying to think rationally. Inevitably, I was soon in a public house. I drank a lot of whiskey and finally went home to my digs. The next morning I was very sick indeed from this terrible mixture of drink and worry. Was the Kelly affair merely a fancy, a drunken fancy? No, there was no consolation in that sort of hope. He was dead all right.

It was as I lay in bed there, shaking, thinking, and smoking, that the mad idea came into my head. No doubt this sounds incredible, grotesque, even disgusting, but I decided I would treat Kelly the same as any other dead creature that found its way to the workshop.

Once one enters a climate of horror, distinction of degree as between one infamy and another seems slight, sometimes undetectable. That evening I went to the workshop and made my preparations. I worked steadily all next day. I will not appall the reader with gruesome detail. I need only say that I applied the general technique and flaying pattern appropriate to apes. The job took me four days at the end of which I had a perfect skin, face and all. I made the usual castings before committing the remains of, so to speak, the remains, to the furnace. My plan was to have Kelly on view asleep on a chair, for the benefit of anybody who might call. Reflection convinced me that this would be far too dangerous. I had to think again.

A further idea began to form. It was so macabre that it shocked even myself. For days I had been treating the inside of the skin with the usual preservatives—cellulose acetate and the like—thinking all the time. The new illumination came upon me like a thunderbolt. *I would don his skin and, when the need arose, BECOME Kelly!* His clothes fitted me. So would his skin. Why not?

Another day's agonised work went on various alterations and adjustments but that night I was able to look into a glass and see Kelly looking back at me, perfect in every detail except for the teeth and eyes, which had to be my own but which I knew other people would never notice.

Naturally I wore Kelly's clothes, and had no trouble in imitating his unpleasant voice and mannerisms. On the second day, having "dressed," so to speak, I went for a walk, receiving salutes from newsboys and other people who had known Kelly. And on the day after, I was foolhardy enough to visit Kelly's lodgings. Where on earth had

I been, his landlady wanted to know. (She had noticed nothing.) What, I asked—had that fool Murphy not told her that I had to go to the country for a few days? No? I had told the good-for-nothing to convey the message.

I slept that night in Kelly's bed. I was a little worried about what the other landlady would think of my own absence. I decided not to remove Kelly's skin the first night I spent in his bed but to try to get the rest of my plan of campaign perfected and into sharper focus. I eventually decided that Kelly should announce to various people that he was going to a very good job in Canada, and that he had sold his business to his assistant Murphy. I would then burn the skin, I would own a business and—what is more stupid than vanity!—I could secretly flatter myself that I had committed the perfect crime.

Need I say that I had overlooked something?

The mummifying preparation with which I had dressed the inside of the skin was, of course, quite stable for the ordinary purposes of taxidermy. It had not occurred to me that a night in a warm bed would make it behave differently. The horrible truth dawned on me the next day when I reached the workshop and tried to take the skin off. *It wouldn't come off!* It had literally fused with my own! And in the days that followed, this process kept rapidly advancing. Kelly's skin got to live again, to breathe, to perspire.

Then followed more days of terrible tension. My own landlady called one day, inquiring about me of "Kelly." I told her I had been on the point of calling on *her* to find out where I was. She was disturbed about my disappearance—it was so unlike me—and said she thought she should inform the police. I thought it wise not to try to dissuade her. My disappearance would eventually come to be accepted, I thought. My Kelliness, so to speak, was permanent. It was horrible, but it was a choice of that or the scaffold.

I kept drinking a lot. One night, after many drinks, I went to the club for a game of snooker. This club was in fact one of the causes of Kelly's bitterness towards me. I had joined it without having been aware that Kelly was a member. His resentment was boundless. He thought I was watching him, and taking note of the attentions he paid the lady members.

On this occasion I nearly made a catastrophic mistake. It is a simple fact that I am a very good snooker player, easily the best in that club. As I was standing watching another game in progress awaiting my turn for the table, *I suddenly realised that Kelly did not play snooker at all!* For some moments, a cold sweat stood out on Kelly's brow at the narrowness of this escape. I went to the bar. There, a garrulous lady (who thinks her unsolicited conversation is a fair exchange for a drink) began talking to me. She remarked the long absence of my nice Mr. Murphy. She said he was missed a lot in the snooker room. I was hot and embarrassed and soon went home. To Kelly's place, of course.

Not embarrassment, but a real sense of danger, was to be my next portion in this adventure. One afternoon, two very casual strangers strolled into the workshop, saying they would like a little chat with me. Cigarettes were produced. Yes indeed, they were plain-clothes-men making a few routine inquiries. This man Murphy had been reported missing by several people. Any idea where he was? None at all. When had I last seen him? Did he seem upset or disturbed? No, but he was an impetuous type. I had recently reprimanded him for bad work. On similar other occasions he had threatened to leave and seek work in England. Had I been away for a few days myself? Yes, down in Cork for a few days. On business. Yes . . . yes . . . some people thinking of starting a natural museum down there, technical school people—that sort of thing.

The casual manner of these men worried me, but I was sure they did not suspect the truth and that they were genuinely interested in tracing Murphy. Still, I knew I was in danger, without knowing the exact nature of the threat I had to counter. Whiskey cheered me somewhat.

Then it happened. The two detectives came back accompanied by two other men in uniform. They showed me a search warrant. It was purely a formality; it had to be done in the case of all missing persons. They had already searched Murphy's digs and had found nothing of interest. They were very sorry for upsetting the place during my working hours.

A few days later the casual gentlemen called and put me under arrest for the wilful murder of Murphy, of myself. They proved the charge in due course with all sorts of painfully amassed evidence, including the remains of human bones in the furnace. I was sentenced to be hanged. Even if I could now prove that Murphy still lived by shedding the accursed skin, what help would that be? Where, they would ask, is Kelly?

This is my strange and tragic story. And I end it with the thought that if Kelly and I must each be either murderer or murdered, it is perhaps better to accept my present fate as philosophically as I can and be cherished in the public mind as the victim of this murderous monster, Kelly. He *was* a murderer, anyway.

After Hours (1967)

by Brian O'Nolan

At ten o'clock on week nights, at half-nine on Saturday the tide ebbs suddenly, leaving the city high and dry. Unless you are staying at an hotel or visiting a theatre, you may not lawfully consume excisable liquors within the confines of the county borough. The city has entered that solemn hiatus, that almost sublime eclipse known as The Closed Hours. Here the law, as if with true Select Lounge mentality, discriminates sharply against the poor man at the pint counter by allowing those who can command transport and can embark upon a journey to drink elsewhere till morning. The theory is that all travellers still proceed by stage-coach and that those who travel outside become blue with cold after five miles and must be thawed out with hot rum at the first hostelry they encounter by night or day. In practice, people who are in the first twilight of inebriation are transported from the urban to the rural pub so swiftly by the internal combustion engine that they need not necessarily be aware that they have moved at all, still less comprehend that their legal personalities have undergone a mystical transfiguration. Whether this system is to be regarded as a scandal or a godsend depends largely on whether one owns a car. At present the city is ringed round with these "bona-fide" pubs, many of them well-run modern houses, and a considerable amount of the stock-in-trade is transferred to the stomachs of the customers at a time every night when the sensible and just are in their second sleeps. . . .

To go back to the city: it appears that the poor man does not always go straight home at ten o'clock. If his thirst is big enough and he knows the knocking formula, he may possibly visit some house where the Demand Note of the Corporation has stampeded the owner into a bout of illicit after-hour trading. For trader and customer alike, such a life is one of excitement, tiptoe, and hush. The boss's ear, refined to shades of perception far beyond the sensitiveness of any modern aircraft detector, can tell almost the inner thoughts of any policeman in the next street. At the first breath of danger all lights are suddenly doused and conversation toned down, as with a knob, to vanishing point. Drinkers reared in such schools will tell you that in inky blackness stout cannot be distinguished in taste from Bass and that no satisfaction whatever can be extracted from a cigarette unless the smoke is seen. Sometimes the police make a catch. Here is the sort of thing that is continually appearing in the papers:

Guard —— said that accompanied by Guard —— he visited the premises at 11.45 P.M. and noticed a light at the side door. When he knocked the light was extinguished, but he was not admitted for six minutes. When defendant opened eventually, he appeared to be in an excited condition and used bad language. There was nobody in the bar but there were two empty pint measures containing traces of fresh porter on the counter. He found a man crouching in a small press containing switches and a gas-meter. When he attempted to enter the yard to carry out a search, he was obstructed by the defendant, who used an expression. He arrested him, but owing to the illness of his wife, he was later released.

Defendant—Did you give me an unmerciful box in the mouth?

Witness—No.

Defendant—Did you say that you would put me and my gawm of a brother through the back wall with one good haymaker of a clout the next time I didn't open when you knocked?

Witness—No.

Justice—You look a fine block of a man yourself. How old are you?

Defendant—I'm as grey as a badger, but I'm not long past forty. (Laughter.)

Justice—Was the brother there at all?

Defendant—He was away in Kells, your worship, seeing about getting a girl for himself. (Laughter.)

Justice—Well, I think you could give a good account of yourself.

Witness—He was very obstreperous, your worship.

Witness, continuing, said that he found two men standing in the dark in an outhouse. They said they were there "for a joke." Witness also found an empty pint measure in an outdoor lavatory and two empty bottles of Cairnes.

Defendant said that two of the men were personal friends and were being treated. There was no question of taking money. He did not know who the man in the press was and did not recall having seen him before. He had given strict instructions to his assistant to allow nobody to remain on after hours. There was nobody in the press the previous day as the gas-man had called to inspect the meter. The two Guards had given him an unmerciful hammering in the hall. His wife was in ill-health, necessitating his doing without sleep for three weeks. A week previously he was compelled to send for the Guards to assist in clearing the house at ten o'clock. He was conducting the house to the best of his ability and was very strict about the hours.

Guard —— said that the defendant was a decent hard-working type but was of an excitable nature. The house had a good record.

Remarking that the defendant seemed a decent sort and that the case was distinguished by the absence of perjury, the justice said he would impose a fine of twenty shillings, the offence not to be endorsed. Were it not for extenuating circumstances he would have no hesitation in sending the defendant to Mountjoy for six months. He commended the Guards for smart police work.

Not many publicans, however, will take the risk. If they were as careful of their souls as they are of their licences, heaven would be packed with those confidential and solicitous profit-takers and, to please them, it might be necessary to provide an inferior annex to paradise to house such porter-drinkers as would make the grade.

Slattery's Sago Saga
OR
From Under the Ground to the Top of the Trees

[An unfinished novel by Flann O'Brien, c.1964–66]

Part One

1

"A bleeding Scotchman, by gob!"

Tim Hartigan said the words out loud as he finished the letter and half turned in his chair to look at Corny, who lifted his head sideways and seemed to roll his eyes.

Tim was wise in a Timmish way. It had perhaps not been wise to have stuffed the letter into his back pocket five days earlier and forgotten about it but that was because he was not used to getting letters and anyway he had been on his way to feed the pigs when Ulick Slattery, the postman, handed it to him. On this morning a strange enlightenment made him think of it and it was wise of him, when he pulled it out at breakfast, to examine first the stamp and postmark very carefully. Yes, it read Houston, Texas, U.S.A. It was also correct of him when he tore the letter open to look at the end of it immediately, to verify that it was from Ned Hoolihan.

Abstractedly, before reading it he had propped the letter against the handsome pewter milk jug and from the little rack of solid silver with 22-carat gold filigree (an article thought to be Florentine), he picked a slice of dry toast, generously buttered it, and rammed a piece between his solid nerveless molars. He lifted his cup of blackish tea and swallowed with echoing gulps. His bland life, he suddenly feared, was about to be disturbed. Could he handle this stranger?

Tim Hartigan, left an orphan at the age of two by his widowed mother, had been adopted when he was four by the high-minded Ned Hoolihan whose cousin, Sister M. Petronilla, was Mother Abbess at the Dominican Home of the Holy Refuge at Cahirfarren. Hoolihan had taken a fancy to the little boy, and that was all about it. He was a wealthy man and brought his new prize home with his baggage to his mansion, Poguemahone Hall. And himself ever of plain habits he had sent Tim not to a college but to the local National School, with a housekeeper at the Hall to look after the boy's other needs.

Before returning to Tim that morning and his letter, it is right to add here a little more about Ned Hoolihan. His money had been mostly inherited as a result of a fortune his father had amassed from automotive and petrol-engine inventions. Indeed, it was a family tradition that Constantine Hoolihan, B.E., had been shamelessly swindled by Henry Ford I but that, through his invention of a primitive computer nourished with a diet of stock-market minutiae, the resourceful engineer from Bohola, Mayo, had managed to get together a sum even bigger than that of which he had been deprived. His only son Ned did not follow this example of thinking out new things, machines, devices, fresh ways of mechanically alleviating the human lot: he was serious, studious, took an early interest in the countryside, God's opulent extemporising, and the great mystery of Agriculture. His doctorate at Dublin University was won on a dissertation (never published) entitled *The Stratification of Alkaline Humus*, thought to be a system of providing natural fertiliser through the deliberate cultivation of fields of weeds for the production of compost and silage, a scheme of tillage in which stray growths of wheat or leek or turnip would be a noxious intrusion.

When he bought Poguemahone Hall, a late Norman foundation of fairly good land in the west, his role became that of gentleman farmer and experimenter in root and cereal crops, aided by his stepson (for he called him that), Tim Hartigan. But after Ned Hoolihan had become an accomplished and scientific seedsman, he found the small farmers and peasants all about him an intractable lot. Instead of sowing "Earthquake Wonder," a Hoolihan seed-potato of infinite sophistication and vigour, made available to them for almost nothing, they persisted in putting down bastardised poor-cropping strains which were chronically subject to scab, late blight, fusoria, and dread rhizoctania canker (or black scurf). The mild, intellectual agronomist almost lost his temper with them outright. But after some years of tuberose planting and preaching to little effect, his patience finally did give out at their rejection of his miraculously healthy and bounteous seed-wheat, "Faddiman's Fancy," for which he had received a citation and praemium from the United States Government. The peasants simply preferred seed of their own domestic procurement, regarding outbreaks of black stem rust, bunt (or stinking smut) as the quaint decisions of Almighty God.

Ned Hoolihan put his affairs in businesslike train, appointed Tim Hartigan his steward at a decent salary, and emigrated to Texas.

There he bought 7,000 acres of middling land, ploughed and fertilised most of it, and put in under Faddiman's Fancy. The rumour was (though never confirmed to Tim in a letter) that he had married about that time. When the young crop was coming up nicely, several dirty black eruptions disfigured the farmlands. Vile as this discolouration looked, it was found on closer inspection to be oil. And Farmer Hoolihan had become unbelievably wealthy.

And now Tim Hartigan was scanning the letter. If it was curt, it was the curtness of affection.

> Dear Tim—By the time you get this you will probably have a visitor, Crawford MacPherson, a dear friend of mine. Take away all the dust-sheets, protective stoves, and rat poisons from my own quarters and make my place available and comfortable for Crawford. If you receive orders, obey them as coming from me.
>
> The Lord be praised, these oil-wells of mine are making so much money that I've lost count. There are 315 derricks standing just now, and I have formed the Hoolihan Petroleum Corporation ("H.P."). Naturally the politicians are moving in but I think I have their measure. Give my regards to Sarsfield Slattery, to the doctor and other neighbours. I enclose extra money.
>
> —Ned Hoolihan

Well, well. Tim sat back and thoughtfully filled his pipe. Would this damn Scotchman wear kilts, maybe play the bagpipes and demand his own sort of whisky? But that was bogus, music-hall stuff, like Americans calling an Irishman a boiled dinner and having him wear his pipe in the ribbon of his hat. Very likely this Scot was just another globe-trotter, very well off, in search of snipe or grouse or some other stuff . . . salmon, perhaps. And Sarsfield Slattery? Tim would have to show that letter to Sarsfield, a friend who occupied a position strangely very similar to his own at neighbouring Sarawad Castle where the wealthy owner, Doctor the Hon. Eustace Baggeley, was in permanent residence. It would be true to add, though, that the Doctor was often away in the sense that he was in the habit of taking strange drugs prescribed by himself. Morphine, heroin, and mescaline had been mentioned but Sarsfield believed that the injections were a mixture of the three, plus something else. Like Ned Hoolihan, the Doctor was also a pioneer of a kind. And, again like Ned Hoolihan, he had adopted Sarsfield, another orphan and born in Chicago, when he was attending a medical conference in that city on the extraction by cattle of a toxic hypnotic drug from hay imported from Mexico.

After Tim had cleared away his breakfast things and washed the dishes, he went up the stone stairs, accompanied by Corny, to refurbish the Boss's quarters, array the great four-poster bed in clean linen, sweep floors, dust the handsome sittingroom, light fires and pull the chain in the lavatory. In the bathroom he thoughtfully laid out some spare shaving gear of Ned's, and even put a fishing rod and unloaded shotgun leaning in a corner of the sittingroom. Orders were orders, and Crawford MacPherson would not only be welcome but would be made feel he was genuinely welcome. It was time, Tim said to himself, that he did a little real work for a change—for he was a conscientious young man. And taking counsel with Sarsfield would have to wait for a little bit.

The forenoon passed quickly and it was about two o'clock in the early autumn day when Tim sat down to his heaped dinner of cabbage, bacon, pulverised sausage, and sound boiled potatoes of the breed of Earthquake Wonder—with *Jude the Obscure* by Thomas Hardy propped up against the milk jug. Corny dined noisily on a large ham-bone which originally bore rags of meat. Some people, Tim reflected as he finished his food, thought Hardy a rather repressed and dismal writer, more taken with groans than lightness of the heart. Well, he was long-winded all right but the problems he faced were serious, they were human questions, deep and difficult, and the great Wessex novelist had brought to them wisdom, solace, illumination, a reconciliation with God's great design. And he had re-peopled the English countryside. The volume itself was the property of Mr. Hoolihan.

A grinding metallic noise came from the courtyard and, looking through the thick distorting glass of the narrow window, Tim saw the leading part of the bonnet of a large motor car. He knew a good deal about cars, and had driven and looked after a Lancia when Ned Hoolihan was in residence.

"Humph," he muttered. "A Packard. Ex-inventory for years. Drive a Packard and proclaim yourself an old man."

But he sat there, unmoved. Could this be the Scotchman? Or maybe a manure vendor? Corny growled softly. Whoever it was, he could knock, no matter if the door was only the tradesman's entrance. Even if it was Jude the Obscure he could knock.

But there was no knock.

The door was noisily flung inward and framed in the entrance was an elderly woman clad in shapeless, hairy tweeds, small red-rimmed eyes glistening in a brownish lumpy face that looked to Tim like the crust of an apple-pie. The voice that came was harsh, and bedaubed with that rumbling colour which comes from Scotland only.

"My name is Crawford MacPherson," she burred rudely, "and am I to understand that you are Tom Hartigan?"

"Tim."

"Tom?"

"Tim!"

"Whatever your name is, tell that crossbred whelp to stop showing his teeth at me."

"My name is Tim Hartigan, the dog's is Corny, ma'am, and both of us are harmless."

She moved forward a few steps.

"Don't you dare to call me ma'am. You may call me MacPherson. Have the manners to offer me a chair. Have you no respect for weemen or are you drunk?"

As Tim Hartigan rose, *Jude the Obscure* fell from his fingers to the floor.

2

Perhaps it was a result of Tim Hartigan's alacrity and good humour, but Crawford MacPherson's mood softened somewhat to one which, though still formidable, was not ferocious. From her big handbag she took a flat silver flask and from it poured yellowish liquid into an empty glass on Tim's table. Corny affected a watchful sleep and Tim, busy loading his pipe, had taken a seat on a chair near the window. MacPherson was looking round what once upon a time had been a considerable kitchen, and grimacing as she sampled her drink.

"How are things going on here?" she asked at last.

"Well, ma'am . . . MacPherson, I mean . . . going on pretty all right. They are nearly ready for harvest, we have three heifers—two of them milkers—ten bullocks, fifty-five sheep, a saddle horse, three tractors, about twenty-five tons of turf and timber, a few good farm workers, and there is a shop about a mile away for groceries, newspapers, fags and that sort of thing. . . . And there's a telephone here but it's usually out of order."

"I suppose you think that's very satisfactory?"

"Well . . . I suppose things could be worse. The owner, Mr. Hoolihan, has made no complaints."

"Oh, is that so? Do you tell me that?"

Here Crawford MacPherson seemed to frown balefully at the floor.

"I think that's the truth," Tim replied rather lamely, "but it's only rarely that I get a letter from him."

MacPherson put her glass down noisily.

"Let me tell you something about Mr. Edward Hoolihan, Hartigan," she said sternly. "I'm his wife."

"Good Lord!" cried Tim, colouring.

"Yes," she continued, "and don't you dare call me Mrs. Hoolihan. I am not compelled by civil or Presbyterian canon law to make a laughing-stock of myself with a title the like of that."

Tim shifted uneasily in his chair, his mind in disarray.

"Aw, well . . . I know," he began.

"I'm over here to put into effect a scheme of my own which, however, has my husband's full approval. There is, of course, no limit to the amount of money I can spend. Mr. Hoolihan thinks that nothing can be done about the peasants of this confounded country. Well, about that, we shall see. *We shall see!*"

Tim Hartigan could suspect storm clouds in his future; some thunder. Even lightning, perhaps.

"Mr. Hoolihan," he said gently, "had some trouble with them himself some years ago. He found them too conservative. He offered them good advice and material help in agriculture but, bedamn it, they wouldn't take it. You see, they're stick-in-the-muds, MacPherson."

"Ah," she said, taking another sup from her glass, "stick-in-the-muds? Yes, they had no time for Earthquake Wonder, I'm told. I'll tell you this much. Stick-in-the-muds they may be, but my business here is to make sure that it is in their own mud they will stick. Understand me? *In their own mud!*"

"Yes. They're unlikely to want to do anything else."

Crawford MacPherson rose, strode to the range where a fire glowed, and turned her back to it, standing menacingly in her brown brogues.

"What they want or don't want is not the important thing, Hartigan. It wasn't, in the past, when a terrible potato famine swept through the country like the judgment of God, about 1846."

"Ah well," Tim ventured, "that was in the dim dark days in the long ago, before we had the good fortune to have Earthquake Wonder in the world."

MacPherson shook her forefinger in anger.

"The people of this country," she thundered, "live on potatoes, which are 80 per cent water and 20 per cent starch. The potato is the lazybones' crop and when it fails, people die by the million. They are starving . . . and they try to eat nettles . . . and straw . . . and bits of stick, and they still die. But a more terrible thing than that happened last century. . . ."

"Heavens above," Tim cried, "what worse calamity than that could occur?"

"The one that *did* occur. They didn't all die. Over a million of those starving Irish tinkers escaped to my adopted country, the United States."

"Thank God," Tim murmured devoutly.

"Yes, you can thank your God. They very nearly ruined America. They bred and multiplied and infested the whole continent, saturating it with crime, drunkenness, illegal corn liquor, bank robbery, murder, prostitution, syphilis, mob rule, crooked politics and Roman Catholic Popery."

"Well, the Lord be praised," gasped Tim, staggered by the violence and suddenness of this outburst.

"Adultery, salacious dancing, blackmail, drug peddling, pimping, organising brothels, consorting with niggers and getting absolution for all their crimes from Roman Catholic priests. . . ."

Tim frowned.

"Well, a lot of other foreigners emigrated to the States," he said. "Germans, Italians, Jewmen . . . even those Dutchmen in baggy trousers."

"People from the European mainland are princes compared with the dirty Irish."

"Oh, I say," Tim cried.

He was angry but his feeling of dismay and being at a loss for a devastating answer was greater. How could he deal with this tartar? Was she off her head?

She unexpectedly returned to the chair at the table and plopped down. She drained the remnant in her glass.

"However," she said, "I don't expect you to understand these matters or know how serious they are. You were never in the United States."

Tim coloured deeply and struck his chair-arm.

"Madam, neither was Saint Patrick."

She opened her bag, produced American cigarettes and lit one.

"I will give you an outline," she said, "of the special business that brings me here. The plan will take considerable time to carry out, and I expect your co-operation and assistance. The object is to protect the United States from the Irish menace. The plan will be very costly but I have so much money from Texas oil at my disposal that I fear no difficulty on that score. My first step will be to buy and nominally take over all Irish agricultural land."

Tim raised his eyebrows, looking sour.

"That would be the highroad to trouble in this country," he said.

"That famine was partly due to rackrenting and absentee landlordism. The people formed an organisation known as the Land League. One man they took action against was Captain Boycott. That's where the word boycott comes from."

But MacPherson, unenlightened, pulled at her cigarette thoughtfully.

"Don't imagine for a moment, Hartigan," she said in her hard voice, "that I intend to get myself embroiled in Irish politics. If I had any taste in that direction, I would not have to leave America to indulge it. I will buy the land and then let it back to the tenants at a nominal rent. A rent of perhaps a shilling a year."

"A *shilling* a year an acre?"

"No. A shilling a year for every holding no matter what the size."

"Well, holy Saint Paul," Tim muttered in wonder, "that would make you out to be the soul of generosity altogether, an angel in disguise from the Garden of Eden."

MacPherson gave a bleak smile.

"There will be one condition, a strict condition. They will not be allowed to grow potatoes."

"But what are the unfortunate people to live on?"

"What they've always lived on. Starch."

Tim puckered his cheeks in a swift inaudible intake of breath. What a strange spectre of a woman this was, to be sure! Where would her equal be found in the broad wideness of the world?

"There is one thing even more productive of starch than the potato," she went on. "And that is sago."

"What? *Sago?*"

"Yes—sago. Do you know what sago is, Hartigan?"

Tim frowned, ransacking his untidy mind.

"Well . . . sago . . . is a sort of pudding, full of small little balls . . . like tapioca. I suppose it's a cereal, the same as rice. And maybe it is subject to its own diseases, like the spud . . . ?"

Again MacPherson's wintry smile came.

"Sago," she said with a minute sort of civility, "is not like tapioca, is not a grain, and will stay free of all disease if its growth is watched. Sago comes from a tree, and the sago tree takes between 15 and 20 years to mature before it can yield its copious, nourishing, lovely bounty."

Tim stared at his boots. The proposition itself was extraordinary, the time complication incredible.

"I see," he said untruthfully.

"The plan is big," MacPherson conceded reasonably, "but in essence reasonable and simple."

"All the same," Tim ventured, "I think you would have to see the Government about it."

"Well, you *are* smart," MacPherson said, almost pleasantly. "That has already been largely taken care of. The American Ambassador in this country has had his instructions. He will shortly inform the Government here that the immigration of Irish nationals to the United States will be prohibited until the cultivation of potatoes in this country is totally banned."

Tim suspected he could detect faint suffusion of perspiration about his brow. He was upset by the velocity of coming events, unless the lady was trying to be funny.

"Well now," he said at last, "suppose you get all this land as you say, and have the sowing of potatoes declared a crime—"

"Then," MacPherson interrupted, "there never again will be a potato famine, and never will there be another invasion of the United States by the superstitious thieving Irish."

"Yes, I know. But you said it takes a sago tree up to twenty years to be any use. What in the name of God are the people to live on during that long time?"

Again came the smile, small but icy.

"Sago," she said.

Tim Hartigan groaned.

"I know I'm stupid but I don't understand."

"Of course I foresaw the question of that gap and have, of course, taken the necessary steps. Beginning in about eight months, my fleet of new sago tankers will ply between Irish ports and Borneo. There are boundless sago reserves, all over the East Indies—in Sumatra, Java, Malacca, Siam and even in South America the cabbage palm is very valuable for sago. Soon you will see sago depots all over this country."

Tim nodded, but frowning.

"Suppose the people just don't like sago, like me?"

A very low, unmusical laugh escaped from MacPherson.

"If they prefer starvation they are welcome."

"Well, how will you get this sago plantation going?"

"Sago trees will grow anywhere, and two freighters loaded with shoots will arrive shortly. A simple Bill in your Parliament expropriating the small farmers and peasants can be passed quickly, with a guarantee that there will be no evictions, or at least very few. You are a young man, Hartigan. You will probably live to see your native land covered with pathless sago forests, a glorious sight and itself a guarantee of American health, liberty, and social cleanliness."

She stood up with some suggestion of conclusion.

"Well, I must get myself fixed up here," she said. "Hartigan, will you bring in my horse?"

Tim turned pale. He had already seen from his narrow window that a narrow horsebox was fastened to the rear of the Packard car and had been wondering about it. Surely it must be a pony?

"To the stables, do you mean?" he asked.

"No, in here. I always like to have my horse near the fire."

Tim got up silently and went out. There seemed to be no limit to this woman's excesses. That night or the following day he would have to get a cable off to Ned Hoolihan for confirmation of these mouthfuls and occurrences, and the assertion that this woman was in fact his wife. He could not have himself made a fool of, or the house destroyed by a lunatic.

A sliding iron vertical bar with bolt at the back of the horsebox was quickly undone and, as the doors opened, Tim's eyes encountered a number of tall, round, smooth, wooden poles, apparently in some way fastened together.

"A clothes-horse by the holy Peter," he muttered.

He blessed himself, pulled out the apparatus, half-shouldered it and staggered towards the house. In the kitchen he pulled it apart so that it stood up.

"That's a good man," said MacPherson in genuine approval.

"I must tell you," said Tim, collapsing to his chair, "that I had a letter from Mr. Hoolihan notifying me of your approaching visit and asking me to have his own quarters upstairs made ready for your occupation. I've done that. Your bed is ready and there's a fire in your bedroom. Do you like sausages for your breakfast?"

"Certainly not. My usual breakfast is oaten porridge followed by sago and cream, and with brown bread and country butter."

Tim managed to nod amiably.

"Well," he smiled, "this place we are in is really the kitchen, and more or less where I live myself. Now, this horse. Shall I bring it up to your own fire?"

MacPherson's eyes wandered about the floor in thought.

"Em, I'm not sure. Leave it here for tonight. Get my travelling bag from my car and then show me to my . . . my flat. I'll give you a bag of sago."

Tim Hartigan did as he was bid. His new charge made no comment at all on Ned Hoolihan's opulent suite but made straight for the lavatory, suggesting to Tim that she had been told where it and everything else was. He scratched his head and stumbled down the stairs, clutching a bag of sago.

"Must get on to Sarsfield as soon as absolutely possible," he whispered to himself. "Else I'm absolutely shagged."

3

"Well, I'm sorry for your trouble, Tim."

Sarsfield Slattery was standing with his backside outwardly poised towards a great log fire, his feet on a rug of thin brown ropes, knitted by himself. He was of smallish structure, thin, with moppy fair hair; sharp, perky features were lit up with narrow, navy-blue eyes, and his peculiar way of speaking with jerky accent and intonation was permanent evidence that he had been born in the northern part of Ireland and was to that extent a sort of disguise, for he had been born in Chicago. The air he carried with him, whether he liked it or not, was one of ineffable cuteness and circumspection. Strangers knew that they had to be very wary with Sarsfield.

It was noon on the rainy morrow. Tim Hartigan lolled sadly in a cane chair, having given Sarsfield a full account of Crawford MacPherson's arrival the preceding day, and what she had said. The recital made things appear much worse even than they had been and, indeed, a lorry had arrived that morning with bags and parcels for the lady, contents undisclosed.

"Weemen," Sarsfield added, "can be wee reptiles, do you know."

Tim had just lit his pipe and looked thoughtful.

"I'm not a windy sort of fellow as you know, Sarsfield," he said, "but I don't like the idea of being by myself with *her* in that house. God knows what she'd turn around and do."

"You can lock the kitchen at night, can't you?"

"At night? Couldn't she get funny ideas during the day?"

"What sort of funny ideas?"

"Couldn't she walk down the stairs without a stitch on her?"

"Ah, I wouldn't say she's that sort."

"Or write and tell Ned that I came up with her tray in the evening and me ballock-naked?"

"Ned wouldn't swally that sort of story," Sarsfield said, grimacing as he pulled at his ear. He paused.

"Tell you the truth, I think Ned must have been floothered when he married that one, and then shipped her out of the States as soon as he could to get shut of her. Too bad that you are left holding the baby."

"I see," Tim replied gloomily. "And what do you think of this sago business?"

"It's all balls."

"That's just what I think, too. But listen here, Sarsfield, if she does get a bit cracked—a bit more cracked than she is—where am I? I have no witness. Now, if she agreed to live *here* . . . instead?"

Sarsfield's answering look was piercing.

"Holy God, isn't a married woman entitled to live in her husband's home?"

Tim coloured a little.

"I suppose so. I've no proof that she's his wife."

"Hasn't she got a ring? What takes *me* to the fair is your brave notion of unloading her on this house. Haven't we enough trouble here? If you have no thought for me, you would be foolish to take anything for granted about my lord and master, Doctor the Honourable Eustace Baggeley."

"Oh, I know I'd have to consult the Doctor. How is he, by the way?"

"He's happier than ever, which means he's worse. He's taking his doses twice a day now. He is talking about converting this castle into a luxury hotel, and even having a casino here. The tourist trade, you know. He thinks the Americans are very attractive people because, like himself, they all seem to have a lot of money. Not that they spend it, if you ask *me*."

Tim frowned a little, clutching at a wisp of hope.

"Is that so? Faith and he might take an interest in Mrs. MacPherson. Why not? She's the wife of one of his best friends and she says she's absolutely stinking and crawling with money."

"Thank goodness they *are* very good friends," Sarsfield said acidly. "That's a very good reason why the Doctor should keep very far away from that lady."

"Oh, I don't know. The Doctor's not a lady's man, if that's what you mean. What the hell is that hammering, Sarsfield?"

Sharp noises, somewhat muffled but loud enough, were heard from the upper intestines of the Castle.

"Ah, that? That's Billy Colum, the handyman. The Doctor gave him orders to put up a framework of timber all around the walls of the big return-lounge, and cover it all over with teak panelling. He's the job nearly finished, and the lounge ruined. I think that's the first stage in the hotel-casino project."

"Good Lord, Sarsfield."

"Aye. The Doc will destroy himself pumping that stuff into his arm. And I think he gives Billy Colum an odd dart now and again."

"Could I see the Doctor? I think I should tell him about Mrs. Ned. You can be sure she's bound to know of him, Sarsfield. I'd better mark his card."

"Whatever you say, Tim. As far as I know he's above in the library. You know the way. Off you go."

Tim did know the way but paused at the lounge to observe Billy at his extraordinary job. A void about four feet wide remained in a large long apartment without the pale shiny panelling already in place from floor to ceiling, built on a heavy timber framework about a foot from the original ornate walls.

"That's a great feat of intricate construction, Billy," Tim said.

Billy Colum, a wizened, wild-eyed little man, looked about him as if seeing his handiwork for the first time.

"Do you know, Tim," he said in his low hoarse voice, "I think the poor Doc is going a bit batty at last. As well as this how-are-ya, he told me to keep an eye out for any jewels that might be knocking about the Castle. He says they can be picked up anywhere."

"Jewels?"

"Jewels. Big ones."

"Does he ever give yourself any medical treatment?"

"Certainly he does. My rheumatism. He gives me a little painkiller in the arm here. Mind you, he's a good doctor behind it all. How could I lift my arm to use a hammer without him?"

Tim smiled as he moved on.

"A casino will be a great improvement in this part of the world," he remarked.

4

The library at Sarawad Castle wore its name sombrely but correctly. A noble, elongated, high-ceilinged room, it had lofty windows which looked strangely narrow, along the right hand, with a single one at the far end corresponding with the door—all hung with dark red curtains, and on those three sides the dark spines of books rose on shelf after shelf from the floor to the roof. In the middle of the fourth wall was a great mantelpiece of green-veined black marble, with brass fire-dogs at the hearth, and a conflagration of steam coal and logs blazing in the grate. Some chairs and other small furniture stood near the fire and, somewhat removed from it in the upper half of the room, was a wide, low distinguished desk. Between it and the fire was a leather armchair in which sprawled elegantly Doctor the Hon. Eustace Baggeley.

The Doctor was quite stout, with ample black hair plastered down, and a middle parting over his broad head. His clean-shaven fleshy features were rude and genial, and his general air was of that kind of youthfulness which warns the perceptive that the man wearing it cannot be as young as he appears. His dress was seen to be fastidious and expensive as he rose to greet Tim Hartigan.

"My dear boy," his low cultured voice said as he stood up with his hand out, "do please come in and sit down. Well, well, Tim, and how are we?"

Tim smiled, shook hands and sat down.

"I'm very well indeed, Doctor. Nothing to complain about that I can think of."

"That's the stuff. All at cookhouse orders, as we used to say in my Army days. And how is Master Cornelius?"

"Oh, in grand form, Doctor. Still at all-out war with all the rats in the parish."

"Excellent."

"I was over seeing Sarsfield, Doctor, and I thought I'd come up here and have a little chat about a few things. . . ."

"I am delighted that you did, dear boy. Tell me this. Have you had any recurrence of that fibrositic visitation in the region of the groin?"

"No indeed. No sign of that for months."

"I am glad. Let me know at once if there should be any more trouble. I have a new embrocation here, administered subcutaneously, a therapeutic truly miraculous straight from Germany."

Tim spread his hand in polite disclaim.

"Thank God I have no need for anything, Doctor."

"Too rash an asseveration," said Doctor the Hon. Eustace Baggeley, rising and going to a sideboard in the dim recess of the far corner.

"If your health is good, still it cannot be so good that a glass of Locke's of Kilbeggan will not put a fresh gloss on it."

As he handed over the glass with a slight bow, he excused himself for not being able to *chequer les verres* but his kidneys had advised him to abstain for a while. He then passed a little jug of water and sat down again, beaming. Tim recalled hearing that alcohol and strong narcotics were often incompatible. He took a good drink of the strong amber distillate and began to fill his pipe.

"Doctor Baggeley," he said, "I wanted to tell you I've had a visitor."

"A visitor, dear boy?"

"Yes. A very strange one. A Scotch lady."

The Doctor slapped his knee.

"Well, well. Scotch . . . and a lady? Scotland for ever!"

Tim rammed expertly at his pipe-bowl.

"That's not all, Doctor. She's living with me . . . at Poguemahone Hall."

"Dear boy! Well, well, well. *Living* with you . . . ?"

He rose and paced delightedly to the hearth rug.

"Living with you in mortal sin, in the opprobrious bondage of the flesh?"

Tim managed a weak smile.

"No, Doctor, I didn't say that, but that isn't all either."

"Don't tell me, dear friend, that she is a distinguished pianist, or somebody that has come to find the True Cross in the Bog of Allen?"

"No. She says she is Ned Hoolihan's wife!"

The Doctor, taken quite off guard in the midst of his banter, staggered to his seat, collapsed into it and presented to Tim a look of blenched amazement. His eyes stayed wide and motionless.

"Ned . . . married . . . to a Scotch shawlie? Heavenly sweet crucified Redeemer and his Blessed Mother above! You are not taking a rise out of me, dear boy?"

"I don't think so, Doctor. I have no proof but that's what she said. And I think she is telling the truth. Her name is Crawford MacPherson and that's what she wants to be called—not Missus Hoolihan."

The Doctor bowed his head, cradling it in his right hand.

"Dear boy, this is most disturbing but let us keep our heads. I would make a telephone call to Ned tomorrow if we only knew where to find him—the damn fool is always up in aeroplanes all over that dirty Texas oil country. As you know, dear boy, I warned him not to go out there."

"Yes, I remember. It was foolish, but he made a lot of money."

"*Money?* Pfff! He had more than he could use when he was here, and what use is money to a man who gets himself married to a Scotch hawsie from the fish-gutting sheds of Aberdeen?"

Tim demurred a bit.

"I don't care for her, Doctor, but I don't think that she's quite that type. I mean, she's no lady but all the same she's not the low working-class type. She brought a horse with her."

"A horse, Tim? Sacred grandfathers! Why should anybody bring a horse to Ireland, where the brutes are to be found in every hole and corner of the country?"

"It's a wooden horse, a folding affair—I mean a clothes-horse. She made me put this thing in front of my own fire."

Doctor Baggeley reflectively fingered his jaw.

"I see," he mumbled. "Yes. That could—I say could—mean one thing. What we call diuresis."

"What's that, Doctor?"

"Pathological incontinence. Bed-wetting and all that line of country."

Tim was dismayed.

"Good Lord! And my friend, poor Ned. Do you mean, Doctor, that she's going to . . . to dry things at my fire instead of upstairs at her own?"

He gulped savagely at his new drink as Doctor Baggeley had risen to pace the floor once again in thought. He stopped.

"Do you know, my dear friend, whether she has any money with her? That itself would be a test of whether she is really Ned Hoolihan's wife. He is, after all, many times a multi-millionaire, even if it's in dollars."

Tim finished his drink and put his glass on a side table with a click so conclusive that the Doctor absently replenished the glass immediately from the bottle now on the mantelpiece.

"Now listen, Doctor Baggeley," Tim said collectedly. "If you would please sit down there again in your chair, I will tell you all I know about Crawford MacPherson's money and her plans."

"Yes, dear boy."

Obediently he sat down, calming himself, and lit a cigarette.

"According to herself she has money without end, millions and millions of it, all of which she can spend with the approval of Mr. Hoolihan, her husband. It seems she can do what she likes with it but she has a plan, a plan to change the whole face of Ireland."

"Dear me now. And why is that?"

"Because she hates the Irish."

"Well, dear boy, that is true of a lot of other people but there is little they can do about it. What particular reason has she for hating the Irish?"

"Because after the Great Famine many, many years ago when the potato crop failed, America was invaded by a million-and-a-half Irish people, starving emigrants if you like, but they pulled through, settled down, and increased and multiplied."

Doctor Baggeley nodded, admiring Tim's gift of concise exposition.

"Of course it wasn't just this influx itself that annoys Crawford MacPherson. It's what the Irish brought with them and planted in America—things she thinks are terrible and dirty."

"What sort of things, dear boy? Do you mean dancing to the fiddle—the 'Rakes of Mallow,' the 'Stooks of Barley' and 'Drive the Jenny Wren?'"

"No, no, Doctor. She says they brought drunkenness, and kip-shops full of painted women . . . and pox . . . and the Catholic faith."

The Doctor made a clucking noise.

"Upon my word, dear boy, but I would not agree that the Irish were pioneers in these matters at all. And the Catholic Church? Heavens above, don't you and I belong to it? And do you remember President Kennedy?"

"Yes. But Crawford MacPherson does not."

"We have the Knights of Columbanus here, remember. Converting outsiders is their business, and I think they get an indulgence for every soul—forty years and forty quarantines or something of the kind."

Tim shook his head.

"Crawford MacPherson has a plan, Doctor. An amazing long-term plan. She wants to make certain there never will be another Great Famine in Ireland because of a failure of the potato crop—and indeed that might happen because of the scandalous way the people here turned up their noses at Earthquake Wonder."

"How right you are, dear fellow. I have tried more than once to persuade Billy Colum and his friends to make Earthquake poteen. That's the boy that would bend your back and make you sing!"

"But," Tim pursued, "any potato, she says, is mostly starch. She wants to replace the potato here by sago, which gives even more starch and is far more hardy. Sago is grown on trees. She wants to have forests of sago trees all over Ireland. She wants to buy up all the farming land and make sago compulsory."

Slow-mounting amazement and pleasure suffused the large countenance of Doctor the Hon. Eustace Baggeley. He almost sprang from his chair to stand on the hearth rug, bending towards Tim.

"Sago? *Sago?* Ah, dear boy, you bring me back to Sumatra, to my Army days. Sago, by Saint Kevin of Glendalough! My dear boy, the very word sago means *bread*."

"I don't like it, Doctor."

"Ah, you may be confusing it with tapioca. You get tapioca by heating the root of the bitter cassava, a tropical shrub of the spurge family. Starch is produced, certainly, but it has nothing to do with sago. Manioc is another name for tapioca."

"Do you tell me that, Doctor?"

"Yes, my boy. In certain parts of South America, meat and manioc is about the only diet for the natives. And they get by on it, but sago would make men of them."

Tim's face clouded in some wonder.

"Do you think, Doctor, that sago trees could be grown here?"

"Of course, dear boy. Of course. Why not? Haven't we got the Gulf Stream? Heavens above, I am delighted!"

"Delighted?"

"I am charmed. Perhaps it is because I am a military medical man but did you know that the Brazilian Indians discovered that roasting the tubers of cassava would disperse the hydrocyanic acid in the milky white sap?"

"No, but is that why you are delighted?"

"Well, not quite, but the manioc shrub grows quickly anywhere, and kills weeds. My heart, though, is in sago."

Tim pulled at his pipe. He found it rather difficult to pin the Doctor down, and now Crawford MacPherson had been momentarily forgotten. The Doctor had moved to a rather littered medicinal tray on his desk and was genially selecting among the contents.

"My dear boy," he said, "I hope to see again, but in Ireland, the gilded palaces of Siam, the turrets and domes of Malacca and pavements littered with baked cakes of sago . . . ah, the wild, burnished enchantment of the East. . . ."

He had found simultaneously an ampoule and a hypodermic syringe.

"But Crawford MacPherson," Tim urged, "says that growing those trees will take years?"

The Doctor had given himself an injection on the side of the right buttock, putting the needle through the trouser cloth. He then sat down, pleased.

"A sago palm of the right strain, my dear Tim," he said, "can mature in fifteen years."

"Well," Tim rejoined, "she says she is going to import sago to this country in tankers, to feed the people while the trees are growing, and wean them off potatoes!"

The Doctor beamed but his face was slightly vacant, reflective.

"I must immediately meet this interesting and gallant lady, Tim. She would now be in Poguemahone Hall, I suppose. But before I go it is essential that you yourself should be instructed in this new big thing, a thing that will change radically the history of Ireland and later the whole social tilt of Western Europe. Have you ever heard of Marco Polo?"

Another stranger, Tim thought. Wasn't the Scotch lady enough to be going on with for the present?

"I don't think so, sir," he said coolly.

"Well, there are books here. Now let me see. . . ."

He rose and walked steadily to the loaded shelves, searching with his eyes, touching the spines of books with questing finger. Two he took down and paused, looking for a third.

"You see," he said with back still turned, "even if it takes a tree fifteen years or more to mature, *you have only a given ten days or so within which to fell it.* You must fell it when it first breaks into bloom, otherwise all your sago is lost. It all goes to nourish the flowers. Do you understand, my dear boy?"

He had returned to his chair, putting three books on the desk and examining one of them.

"Well, if that's the situation, Doctor," Tim said expansively, "the trees would have to be spread out as to the times of planting, otherwise you could have tens of thousands of trees requiring to be felled almost on the same day... and where would you get the labour in a situation like that?"

The Doctor smiled in approval.

"How very alert you are," he said. "Splendid! I think Ned's good wife will have an able lieutenant in you. Yes. Now I'm marking certain pages and passages in these books with slips of paper. I want you to take a rest here and read those passages: here, I mean, today. And read also any other parts which may appeal to you. You may rely to an unlimited extent in your labours on the produce of Locke's Distillery of Kilbeggan."

He rose, as did Tim also, surprised.

"But," he asked, "what about my new boss at the Hall?"

The Doctor patted his shoulder.

"You need not worry about that at all, my dear boy, for I am now on my way to see her. I will explain that I have asked you to undertake some research that would be dear to her heart. So sit down and relax, and have another drink. On my way down I will see how Billy Colum is getting on with that panelling in the hall. And I'll tell Sarsfield not to disturb you here but to bring you up a tray in a few hours."

Tim Hartigan smiled. He knew this man could be quite impossible but his heart was in the right place.

"Well, thanks, Doctor," he said. "That's very nice of you. I'll do what you say. But I would like you to warn Sarsfield Slattery about one thing."

"What is that?"

"No sago."

"Ah-ha? No sago."

With a wave the Doctor was gone, carrying a very small bag.

5

Tim Hartigan, having picked up the first book, went back to his chair and looked it over. Good large print, he noted with approval. Opening it at the bookmark finally, he laid it face down and attended meticulously to his glass, pouring himself a generous noggin of Locke's medicament, flavouring it slightly with water and then gratefully flushing his gullet downward. No wonder, he reflected, that the old-time monks were great scholars, for they had the wit to make on the premises the medicine that gave the mind ripeness and poise, satisfying the bodily thirst while sharpening the thirst for knowledge on that wine from the butts of God's vineyards of human knowledge.

He eyed the library about him with a friendly eye, then carried his book and vessels to the great desk and thankfully sank into the commodious personal chair of Doctor the Hon. Eustace Baggeley. Then he began his reading.

Sleator's Deposit of Dietetic Cosmography, p. 627:

The true sago palm flourishes in low marshy situations, growing to a maximum height of 30 ft. It matures to yield starch at age 15–20 years.

The whole interior of the stem will then be found to be gorged with spongy medullary matter enclosed by a hard shell—the only wood of the stem. At this stage the tree will be observed to put forth its terminal flowering spikes and after three years these ripen to fruits and seeds. If this is allowed to proceed, the whole starch will have been used up, the stem becomes a hollow shell, and the plant has been killed in that supreme effort. But immediately the flowering spikes appear, the stem is felled, cut up into portions of from 4 to 6 ft. long, and carried off to the factory.

There they are split lengthways, and their medullary starch scooped out. This is thrown into water and washed until all fibrous material and other impurities float to the surface. After standing for a time, the fecula settles on the bottom of the trough, and is successively washed and the water decanted. Then it is dried and constitutes "sago meal."

To prepare for the shops the meal is again moistened and put into bags, in which it can be well shaken and beaten when suspended from the roof of the room.

It is next rubbed over sieves of various mesh until it is separated into "pearl sago," "granulated sago," &c , when it is dried in the open or over ovens.

The refining of sago into the grades required by the European market is done largely by the Chinese in Singapore. . . .

About 1913 the average yearly imports to the United Kingdom of sago, sago meal and sago flour was about 29,000 tons.

* * *

The Book of Marco Polo the Venetian (2 vols.)
by Col. Sir Henry Yule. II, p. 300:

The people have no wheat, but have rice which they eat with milk and flesh. They also have wine from trees such as I told you of. And I will tell you another great marvel. They have a kind of tree that produces flour, and excellent flour it is for food. These trees are very tall and thick but have a very thin bark, and inside the bark they are crammed with flour. And I tell you that Messer Marco Polo, who witnessed all this, related how he and his party partook of this flour made into bread, and found it excellent.

Ibid., pp. 304–5:

An interesting notice of the sago tree, of which Odoric also gives an account; Ramusio is however here fuller and more accurate: "Removing the first bark, which is but thin, you come upon the wood of the tree, which forms a thickness all round of some three fingers, but all inside this is a pith of flour, like that of the Carvolo. The trees are so big that it will take two men to span them. They put this flour into tubs of water, and beat it up with a stick, and then the bran and other impurities come to the top, while the pure flour sinks to the bottom. The water is then thrown away, and the cleaned flour that remains is taken and made into *pasta* in strips and other forms. These Messer Marco Polo often partook of and brought some with him to Venice. It resembles barley bread and tastes much the same. The wood of this tree is like iron, for if thrown into water it goes straight to the bottom. It can be split straight from end to end like a cane. When the flour has been removed the wood remains, as has been said, three inches thick. Of this the people make short lances, not long ones, because they are so heavy that no one could carry or handle them if long. One end is sharpened and charred in the fire and, when thus prepared they will pierce any armour, and much better than iron would do.

* * *

Malay Archipelago 1896 by A. E. Williams:

When sago is to be made, a full-grown tree is selected just before it is going to flower. It is cut down close to the ground, the leaves and leaf-stalks cleared away and a broad strip of the bark taken off the upper side of the trunk. This exposes the pithy matter, which is of a rusty colour near the bottom of the tree, but higher up pure white, about as hard as a dry apple, but with woody fibres running through it about a quarter of an inch apart. The pith is cut or broken down into a coarse powder, by means of a tool constructed for the purpose. . . .

Water is poured on the mass of pith, which is kneaded and pressed against the strainer till the starch is all dissolved and has passed through, when the fibrous refuse is thrown away, and a fresh basketful put in its place. The water charged with sago passes to a trough, with a depression in the centre, where the sediment is deposited, the surplus water trickling off by a shallow outlet. When the trough is nearly full, the mass of starch, which has a slight reddish tinge, is made into cylinders of about thirty pounds' weight, and neatly covered with sago leaves, and in this state is sold as raw sago. Boiled with water, this forms a thick glutinous mass, with a rather astringent taste, and is eaten with salt, limes and chillies. Sago bread is made in large quantities, by baking it into cakes in a small clay oven containing six or eight slits, side by side, each about three-quarters of an inch wide and six to eight inches square. The raw sago is broken up, dried in the sun, powdered, and finely sifted. The oven is heated over a clear fire of embers, and is lightly filled with sago powder. The openings are then covered up with a flat piece of sago bark, and in about five minutes the cakes are turned out sufficiently baked. The hot cakes are very nice with butter, and when made with the addition of a little sugar and grated cocoa-nut, are quite a delicacy. They are soft, and something like corn-flour cakes, but have a slight characteristic flavour which is lost in the refined sago we use in this country. When not wanted for immediate use, they are dried for several days in the sun, and tied up in bundles of twenty. They will then keep for years; they are very hard, and very rough and dry.

Tim closed the book, finished the remains of his drink and thoughtfully re-charged his glass. He frowned a little as he filled his pipe. How could people seriously attempt to live on sago? Is it really a staple, such as bread made from wheaten flour is with us? And would those easterly people think it very odd that the Irish should put such trust in potatoes, even if the potatoes were (as assuredly they were not) Earthquake Wonders? By all accounts the Garden of Eden was not marshy and it was fairly sure that no lofty sago trees there kept off the heat of the sun, any more than Adam and Eve dug the sinless soil for the world's first potatoes. He kindled the pipe and half-closed his eyes in reverie.

The door flew inward with a noise and Sarsfield Slattery hurried inward, alert and frowning a bit.

"Tim, was Billy Colum here?"

"No. Nobody was here. Why?"

"I was bringing him up a cup of tea and a slice of brown bread. The Doctor told me to keep an eye on him. He's gone!"

"*Gone*? Heavens, I was just reading some stuff here about sago to please the Doctor, and, well . . . thinking . . . and drinking. I thought Billy was working away down there."

"Well, he has disappeared off the face of the earth. The Doctor is at your place. I'd better ring him."

Tim nodded helplessly.

"I suppose it would be the wise thing," he agreed.

6

At Poguemahone Hall Tim decided to leave Sarsfield and go up to Crawford MacPherson's private quarters alone. His own life having so swiftly proceeded from simplicity to complexity, he now began to fear boundless confusion and resolved for his own part to be more than careful. What untold things might not result from the collision of the drug-charged Doctor and a foreigner with no right command of her wits? What incomparable things might happen in the house of Ned Hoolihan while the owner was up in an aeroplane mapping his oil empire in Texas or marking the spot of a rogue gusher? Tim knocked on the door and entered.

Doctor the Hon. Eustace Baggeley was elegantly sprawled on the broad sofa, smiling broadly with a gleam in his eyes. Crawford MacPherson was in the armchair by the fire: not annoyed, not genial but seemingly in an acceptable neutral humour.

"Well, Tim, what's the trouble?" she asked.

"My dear boy, you look pale," the Doctor beamed.

Tim ventured to take a seat, for his own ingestion of Locke's had somewhat dissipated his natural reticence.

"I thought I should let you know, Doctor, that your man Billy Colum has disappeared. Sarsfield Slattery missed him and after we searched and shouted for him, we thought we should come over here and let you know right away."

MacPherson put the glass in her hand on the table.

"What's this, Doctor? People disappearing? Innocent bodies being whisked away? I thought things were settled in this country."

The Doctor airily waved a hand.

"My dear Crawford, nothing in this world is ever settled. Billy is a queer little man, full of whims and crucified with rheumatism. He'll probably show up again in a few days. Maybe he has gone to see his old mother in Killoochter. Did he leave a message, Tim?"

"He left nothing, sir. Just disappeared."

MacPherson stood up.

"It seems it is just my misfortune to walk into some sort of criminality at your Castle, Doctor. A thing that smells of agrarian kidnapping, Fenianism or something of the kind. Where are the police? I can ring up the American Ambassador in Dublin if there is a telephone in working order in this unholy district."

The Doctor also rose, intact in his good humour.

"My dear lady, nothing of the kind. Billy is quite harmless, and a first-class carpenter. He was panelling a hallway for me. We don't keep office hours in this country, you know. You never can tell. He might have suddenly remembered that he had to post a letter and there's a two-mile walk in that job."

The lady snorted.

"I have no doubt at all," she said in a hard voice, "that your wretched potatoes inflict weakness in the head as well as in the bones. All the same, he is your workman, Doctor. We had better go and investigate."

"But, my dear Crawford. . . ."

"At once!"

In a surprisingly quick time coats and hats had been got and the company, including Sarsfield Slattery, were getting into the Doctor's aged Bentley. Nothing could disturb his panache and, as the car started, he gave his new passenger caution of what to expect from the unkempt country roads of Ireland, even if the journey was less than a mile.

"I am not a complete tyro, Doctor," she replied. "I got off the liner near Cork and drove up here in my Packard, and it couldn't be worse in the highlands of Kangchenjunga. Why haven't the people here smart ponies and traps instead of those donkey-carts?"

"Ponies," replied the Doctor, "are useless for agricultural labour in the little fields. We need all-purpose animals here, and cars that can carry potatoes and manure as well as people. In my Army days outside Singapore we had ploughing done by cows. Did you ever eat yak butter, Crawford?"

"I did not, sir. I take it you have never heard of sago butter?"

The Doctor laughed.

"Indeed no, but though delicious, like sago cheese, it's hardly as nourishing as cows' butter."

"*Nourishing*? That's the nonsense to be heard from doctors all over the world—*nourishing*. Are potatoes nourishing? The purpose of food is to keep people alive, *and in their own country*. Potatoes are hardly known at all in the States. It is surprising how easy it is for the Irish who get there to forget their native spuds."

"That reminds me," Sarsfield interjected. "Billy Colum missed his dinner."

The Doctor had been driving his gallant old car and was now nearing his own splendid castellated entrance, always hospitably open, with the pushed-back gates permanently immured in stones and bracken.

"Here we are at Sarawad, Crawford. The word sarawad is Gaelic and means 'before long.' A delightful name, you'll agree. It spells out hope, and better times to come."

Looking about her, the lady said:

"There's a lot of loose, foolish talk out of the people here—all of them. The climate may take part of the blame but not all of it. I hope you have a drink in the house, Doctor?"

The Doctor had pulled up and reached for the doors.

"Here we are, madame. Sarawad Castle, home of peerless foodstuffs and the true, the blushful Hippocrene."

Crawford MacPherson did not waste time or admiration on the fine old door or the lofty entrance hall, nor on the gaming weapons and animals' heads which crowded its walls; she seemed to be leading the party, as if she owned the Castle, up the stairs to the lounge which had been the scene of Billy's labours. The artificial walls of teak, flawless and complete, gleamed in the evening light while a chair, a saw, and the neat mess a good carpenter leaves behind were in the middle of the floor.

"He was finishing the job here as I passed down," the Doctor said, tapping a section of the wall. "I gave him a little bit of a hand and he appeared to be his usual good self."

"Was he sober?" MacPherson asked.

"Sober as the day he was born because Billy never touched intoxicating drink. It wasn't that drink was against his rule, or mine either, but it played hell with his rheumatism. You see, his rheumatism was congenital, the poor man. He was a martyr to that disorder but he never complained nor let himself be depressed."

"He offered all his pains up to God," Tim said piously.

MacPherson glowered about the room and from face to face.

"How could a cripple be a carpenter?" she demanded.

"Oh, the Doctor himself looks after him," Sarsfield replied. "He gets by all right, ma'am."

"Don't you dare call me ma'am!"

"You see, Crawford," the Doctor interposed, "his trouble is not really old-fashioned inflammation of the muscles and joint tissue but a verruculose affection of the tendons. Very disabling and discouraging but a dart from me restores him to condition, rather like winding up an alarm clock. You may be sure I look after my staff."

"I see. His muscles are all right but his tendons are permanently wrecked. I imagine that situation would make him worse. Has he been given to disappearing like this?"

"Not really, Crawford," the Doctor replied amiably. "But he takes his own time at a job, and goes about it in his own way. You see, we're a sort of happy family here. Billy Colum was a bit of an artist. You can't hurry a man of that kind—not if you want a proper stylish job done."

"And tell me, Doctor, do those injections sicken or upset him in any way?"

"Yerra not at all. They sometimes make him sing, help to take him out of himself. Help him to get a good night's sleep, too, for he does have a touch of insomnia."

"But does he eat properly?"

"Lord save us," Tim interrupted, "*eat?* He's so hungry most days he'd eat a dead Christian Brother. When Billy sits down he clears the decks. Give him a bucket of Irish stew—potatoes, onion, and any God's amount of meat, boiling hot, and he'll shovel it down the inside of his neck like a man possessed."

MacPherson glared at him.

"You mean, young man, that he is addicted to gluttony? Doctor, could we pay a visit to your own quarters, just the two of us?"

"A pleasure, Crawford."

Tim and Sarsfield looked at each other ruefully as their betters departed. This lady made as little distinction as between persons and classes. She was just as overbearing and peremptory with the Doctor as with them and apparently thought her husband's money had demolished all barriers.

"This ould wan," Sarsfield mused, "is getting a bit on my nerves."

"Is that so, my poor man," Tim rejoined drily. "This is the first time she has been here, possibly the last time. I have to live with her, day and night, and she may be staying at Poguemahone for years—*for years*, man. How would you like changing places with me?"

"I'd rather go to the States, like Hoolihan. But Billy . . . I know that the Doc sometimes gives him a dart of his own needle. Something terrible is going to happen. I didn't hear Billy leave the house, in fact I didn't miss him till I went to call him for his dinner."

"What's all the fuss about?" Tim asked irritably. "He finished his job. He finished his job and maybe decided to slope off for a drink. You heard the Doc say that Billy was a total abstainer? That was a good one."

"Listen, Tim," Sarsfield said earnestly, "you know very well Billy doesn't get ideas of that kind. When he's tired working, and hungry, the only idea in his head is to make a ferocious attack on his dinner. You know that very well."

Tim did not pay much attention, for he was examining and testing the panelling—a job well done, he had to confess, and skillfully.

"Let's hope," he said at last, "that Billy won't be found drowned in a bog hole."

"Does her ladyship let you smoke?" Sarsfield asked.

"What?" Tim rasped. "Me, smoke? I'll smoke my pipe any time and anywhere I want to."

Sarsfield lit a cigarette and pulled gratefully at it, undeterred by returning voices.

"Since you have the instrument, my dear," the Doctor said re-entering, "you might give the chests of those two boys a run over. They are divils for smoking, a thing I personally steer clear of. Any news, boys?"

"Not a thing," Tim said as he noticed that MacPherson was swinging a stethoscope.

"Holy God," muttered Sarsfield, taken aback.

"Show me again, Doctor," MacPherson said briskly, "just where the missing man finished his work."

"Surely," the Doctor replied. "I stopped to talk to him and gave him a slight amateur's helping hand just here, look."

She nodded and, with ear-pieces in place, began to run the bell of the stethoscope over that particular part of the wall, stooping to cover the lower parts. Suddenly she stood upright and wheeled round.

"You," she said sharply to Tim Hartigan, "get a chisel or something and break the panelling away at this seam!"

Frowning, Tim bent among the tools. The Doctor, still jovial but a little concerned, intervened.

"But, my dear, that's finished work—I mean, it would be a pity to break it up."

Tim carefully handed a chisel and hammer to Sarsfield.

"Quite so, Doctor. It would also be a pity for one of your workmen to lose his life."

After a nod from his employer, Sarsfield inserted the chisel-edge at a scarcely perceptible seam and began his crude hammering until rending sounds concluded with a ragged gap torn in the panelling. MacPherson peered in.

"Quick, boy," she cried, "break down some more towards the floor and get him out. He's in there, on his back!"

Confusion of work and voices ensued until Tim found himself behind the panelling dragging the comatose Billy to his feet and manhandling him towards the light of the ope—and final rescue.

"Well, good Lord," the Doctor said, gaping, "how on earth could he build himself into the wall? The tiny nails are driven in from the outside. Goodness me, this is the limit. How do you feel, Billy?"

MacPherson, hands on huge hips, was grim.

"Doctor, did you help him with this job? Did you give him an injection for his tendons?"

Billy was sitting disconsolately on the floor, only partially conscious.

"He's coming to," Sarsfield cried.

"I certainly gave him a little help," the Doctor said pleasantly. "That verruculose affliction could put a delicate job like this all wrong."

"You'd better put this man to bed," MacPherson said to Sarsfield, "and then let us have a rest in your library, Doctor."

"With pleasure, my dear," the Doctor replied with total recall of his good humour. "Those careless little chaps would need somebody to mind them all the time."

At first undecided, Tim followed his principals to the library, happy that he had earlier put away his own books and drinking utensils. MacPherson sat by the fire, putting the stethoscope on the desk while the Doctor produced the Locke's and three—yes, three—glasses. MacPherson drank appreciatively, apparently judging that the situation was one of some small triumph for her.

"My dear Doctor," she said, "forgive me if my manner over this little mystery seemed a bit brusque. But human suffering disturbs me. That is why I feel that the money at my disposal must be applied to the amelioration of man's lot in general."

"By the ingestion of sago, my dear?"

"That is one way, the fundamental way for Ireland. But it is not by any means exclusively a matter of the stomach, of diet, or even of the startling change in the national scenery. With vast countrywide plantations of sago pine there will be, for example, a new wild life in Ireland. . . ."

The Doctor clapped hands.

"My dear girl, how charming! You do excite me. In my Army days—indeed, in all my younger days—the hunt was a preoccupation with me which almost made my work take second place. I never enjoyed shooting at people, matteradamn whether they were niggers or coolies . . . but tigers! Ah!"

MacPherson contrived the ghost of a smile.

"Well, in my own younger days," she said, "researching sago in the wilder parts of Sumatra and the Malay Peninsula, I had to be on my guard against some very large fierce creatures such as the Asiatic elephant, the bison and the rhinoceros, and several kinds of bear. . . ."

"Jolly good, by Jove!"

"But these large mammals would scarcely find sustenance in Ireland, even if they were allowed to kill and eat the people. But the smaller wild animals can be deadlier. The sago rat is indigenous in any territory where the pine grows. The tapir, the sambhur and the siamang, a strange sort of anthropoid ape, will probably appear here. Also the crab-eating macaque, I can see that flourish in Connemara. I would not be sure of the Asiatic tiger and black panther coming here, for they are very wide-ranging and predatory creatures, but many smaller jungle cats and wild boars may be expected. There would be no counting the breeds of alien birds which would roost in the sago pines. . . ."

"Ah, my dear lady—blue partridge, argus pheasant and the cotton teal, I sampled them in the eating-houses of Hong Kong."

"Yes, Doctor, but a thing not to be ignored will be the swarms of new insects, house-monkeys and quadruped snakes and, glory be to God, the din will be something new to this country, particularly at night."

There was a brief silence of reflection.

"Are you sure, my dear Crawford, that this . . . this bouleversement of hemispheres, to so speak, is worthwhile in the mere interest of changing the potato for sago in this country?"

MacPherson put down her empty glass smartly.

"Of course I do. Don't millions of people live under such conditions in the East? What would happen if they were all to decide to emigrate to America?"

"Hmmm. That would be a bad show. Have another drink?"

"Thanks."

"Tim?"

"Thank you, Doctor."

"I must be getting home, Doctor, very soon. I have letters to write and notes to make. So charming meeting you."

The Doctor beamed genuinely.

"Ah, my dear Crawford, for me it has been a supreme pleasure and honour to welcome to these poor parts the wife of my dear friend Edward Hoolihan. I will ask Sarsfield Slattery to drive you home in my car."

"But thank you so much. We will meet again in a few days. I want to talk to you about another most important by-product. I mean sago furniture."

And thus a meeting, so strange in its sequel, came to an end that evening.

7

On reaching Poguemahone Hall, Tim Hartigan parted from the new chatelaine, picked up in the hall an airmail letter addressed to himself and made his way to his kitchen quarters. He was tired, and intestinally a bit irked by spent whiskey. He went to bed, rekindled his pipe and opened the letter.

Dear Tim—It's beginning to be the devil out here. More gushers are blowing their tops about every third day and I don't believe I manage a total of more than 15 hours real sleep a week, quite alone and in perfect peace, peace that was possible only by reserving an entire floor of the Blue Water Gulf Hotel in Corpus Christi with a squad of my own private cops to keep Press and TV scruff away and to block all telephone assaults. It's not that I'm short of assistance and offers of help. Those offers are so continuous and persistent and descending on me from every quarter in such a deluge that my nerves by now are pretty well in flitters. A Jesuit Father, Michael Peter Connors, managed to get himself invited up to breakfast with me on the pretext of getting a sub for a new convent of the Little Sisters of the Stainless Eucharist in Dallas (of course I'm still as much of a sucker for the old Church as ever I was as a simple farmer at Poguemahone) and when he pulled out some sort of an illuminated book for me to sign so that I would be remembered in 10,000 Masses that are to be offered in the convent chapel for benefactors over 25 years from the opening date, a little box of .357 Smith and Wesson slugs fell out into his damn plate of bacon. I knew them and the box because I have one of those rods myself. I pressed a secret buzzer at my foot under the table and when two cops bounced in and frisked my Jesuit he turned out to be a cousin of Congressman Joshua Hedge—a real friend of mine in Washington, I think. This silly bogman didn't plan to shoot me, of course; he just wanted a cheque, no matter a bugger to whom payable, so as to have some notes to play with and maybe buy himself a vacation in Europe. I gave him fifty bucks in notes but warned him I'd give Hedge a prod about him. It looks to me like everybody in this Texas goes about fully armed and any man in the habit of carrying readies in his pocket has a quiet bodyguard about as near to him as his underwear—he wouldn't go to the lavatory without a gunman on guard outside the door. I needn't tell you I carry an old-fashioned Colt 45 myself *and know how to use it*—got lessons and half an hour's practice every day for a fortnight from the Marshal at Fort Worth, a Clareman named O'Grady. I carry a couple of grut balls, too—little bombs about a thousand times worse than tear gas but with no effect on the thrower (yours truly) who takes just one grutomycin tablet every morning. Don't write to me here in Corpus Christi as my GHQ is still Houston. I have moved from the Old Mexico mansion and now have 7 floors in the Houston Statler, and please make a note of that address. George Shagge, the Laredo steel-man, wants me to buy the whole damn hotel and settle in but I don't know, I think I'll wait a bit. Some of my oil tickles in Arizona have suggested that this State is sitting on a bed of uranium and maybe Texas won't be my last home. But I like it here. This territory is so big and so bulging with treasure under the ground that a man feels he's neglecting it just by being in any one place. Oil means hundreds of miles of big-bore pipeline, some to my refinery at Houston and others to new refineries I am putting up at Galveston and Sabine, and also at Pensacola in Alabama—we can't move oil to the west and east coasts except by tanker. The railroads here are all in the hands of crooks. I've taken over a firm making drilling rigs in Tulsa, Oklahoma, for by jiminy I have options on 1,858 sq. miles of fresh territory here in Texas where the tests have been more than good. Total no. of H.P. derricks at work just now is 731. Two fellows I know here are running for Governor in the neighbouring State of New Mexico—Cactus Mike Broadfeet and Harry Poland—and I'm quietly backing both because that's the way business goes here. This whole State is alive with hoodlums and politicians, and when was there any difference between those two classes? I'm as busy as buggery but I'm not slow—I play the Kennedy R.C. ticket and I'll be just another brave U.S. Catholic as soon as my citizenship comes through—Cactus Mike says I'm perfectly right and that this great State of over 7 million souls is entitled to a Cardinal and if he is elected Governor in New Mexico he intends to park some fixers and use money (mine, I presume) in Rome. By God, if he wants to serve the Cross that way, why shouldn't he since he serves or used to serve the fiery cross with the KKK outfit—and now with an election next door there's no shortage of those gunboys in nightshirts putting the fear of Jesus into the niggers. You might think I'm now long enough in the U.S. to have a few friends here and there but honestly, Tim, I'm lonely as hell and have to keep fighting like a Trojan to keep away from the licker. Some of my buddies, as they call themselves, may be all right under the skin but I just don't have the mental machinery to tell which of them are bums or hoods. They have all a profound, sincere, undisguised interest in money—MY money, I'd say—and I needn't tell you they mostly want it to prop up poor prostitutes in homes, teach the alphabet to blind cripples, found new Orders of nigger and octaroon nuns and make absolutely certain that the Democrats will never lose this State. Cactus Mike Broadfeet has a button up certifying he has given 24 pints to the Our Lady of the Lake Blood Bank at San Antonio but maybe the button means he swallows 24 pints of corn licker a week for by God you'd swear his face was on fire. As I think you know, the only way to get about this territory which is bigger than all Germany is by air. I've two machines of my own, a jet and a turbo-prop, but I'm nervous as a kitten up there, even if every flyer and cop I have took an oath on the Douai to play straight. Four of my boys have been shot up in the last 10 months and a girl that types for me got so savagely mugged that the New York hospital that now has her says she'll never walk or stand up again. The mobsters here have no respect whatsoever for womankind. With a State election coming up nearby the night riders have got mighty plentiful and Harry Poland has made the crack on TV that Cactus Mike Broadfeet would be the ideal man for Governor of Oklahoma except that he has trench mouth, his love for the Democrat Party is phoney, he has a bordello in the sacristy of his First American Church of the Plymouth Presbyterians *and* his expectation of life is short—that last a thing Poland has referred to the Attorney as a threat of assassination. Somehow I feel Cactus Mike will pull this thing off because he is a real prairie Texan, owns a big chain of shirt factories through the west coast and the word has been spread that Harry Poland is a Jew from Lithuania, though he wears a holy medal in gold he got from Cardinal Spellman and never touches meat on Friday. He has cotton scrubshops at Austin, Amarillo and El Paso but the boys say his real call is the drug business and that he was linked up with the Mafia outfit Cosa Nostra. He certainly takes snow himself for the good of his health and that's about the colour of his face if not of his soul. Do you know, I'm nearly mad enough to run for the chair of Governor of one of the States here only I'm not a citizen yet. What I DO wish badly is that yourself could come out here and give me a hand at running this big booming oil mess-up but of course you can't with all that important work on your hands back there at Poguemahone. By God though I need a real Irishman out here. Things will be easier later on though, when I get some sort of a real *organisation* working—that's the big, true, business word, ORGANISATION. By the Lord, we have enough juice hereabouts to oil the wheels if only we had the wheels there and organised to turn.

Now Tim I've left to the last the big question never out of the back of my distracted mind these times—*how is my dear wife Crawford?* I'm sure you were pretty shook and maybe annoyed with me for the abrupt way I unloaded her on you without any right warning but Tim, you could say that girl saved my life when this sudden oil strike unbalanced me and drove me straight to the bottle. In three months I was halfway down the river on a tide of bourbon, not even the decent potstill drop you have at home, giving orders in the oil fields, signing options and cheques and hiring and firing without any proper notion of what I was about. God in his mercy saw to it that Crawford was lurking somewhere on my office staff and He inspired her to come to my side, guide my silly hand, save me from myself and get me the best doctors to be had across the whole U.S. and a first-class specialist named Dr Feodor Unterholtz from Austria. She never took her eyes off me nor let anybody else mess me up, and one night even had the nerve to order Cactus Mike out of the house. An angel in disguise if you like but still an angel. And she did not pull back when a direct sacrifice by herself was called for. As you probably know by now she is of stern Presbyterian stock but knew I would never be permanently safe, safe for keeps, unless she married me. You can well imagine the awful struggle that was there in the middle of her soul for of course she knew I was an Irish Catholic and knew the view our sort of people take of the sacrament of marriage. See the hobble she was in? I think she saw Cardinal Spellman or Cardinal Cushing or somebody on the Q.T. but I can tell you this—when the awful choice was put in front of her on a plate, Crawford didn't flinch. No, sirreee! She took instruction from a local P.P., learned her prayers like a Castlebar schoolgirl and behind my back was received into the Church. Another soul for God, Tim—aren't they wonderful, the ways of Providence? I was on tegretol and morphine and benzedrine and the devil knows what but I nearly fell through the middle of the bed when she told me one night everything was fixed. It made a new man of me, invalid and all as I was. I made a novena of thanksgiving to Our Lord and His Blessed Mother, and I don't give a damn how much cynical people will jeer at all the oil and money I have, there was no trouble at all to getting Cardinal Cushing to agree to give us a Solemn Pontifical Nuptial High Mass with Gregorian Choir for the wedding. I arranged a sort of a double-take by having the Mass, wedding ceremony and the reception at the Houston Statler brought live on closed-circuit TV to the New York Hilton where a second simultaneous reception was held, with Senator Hovis Oxter and his wife Bella deputising for myself and bride, and I think you can take it from me that a good time was had by all—or by about 7,500 guests. Our honeymoon at Miami was very brief, of course, and very *careful* indeed with myself on antabus if you know what that drug is for, sweet God the smell of a cork and the poor reformed drinking man is down the Swanee.

I suppose you wonder what I think of Crawford's brainstorm about putting an end for good and all to potato-eating in Ireland. Well, this America is a great country with nothing beyond the boundless horizon only another enormous horizon beckoning on but I still remember very affectionately the land that gave me birth but I may say that the disgraceful way the native peasants treated my Earthquake Wonder still rankles bitterly in my nose. If the Irish don't recognise a sound, decent, bug-free potato when they are offered one, then they don't deserve any potato at all—those are *my* feelings—and they have thoroughly merited the decision to have sago made the national mainstay. Poor Crawford tried to interest myself in sago but nothing in that line has ever agreed with me, though who can say what I would think at my present age if I had had sago from the cradle as the new generation of Irish people probably now will have.

My own conviction and my money are totally behind Crawford's scheme because (one) the extremely delicate and complicated business of handling oil men, geological and mineral technicians, banker and financial panjandrums, to say nothing of State and Federal politicians, *are no proper concern for a decent young married woman*: and (two) my dear wife is finding happiness in the fulfillment of philanthropic yearnings far from home. It is a great pleasure and consolation to me that she should decide to see the bigger world from the resolve, God willing, to improve it and in doing so help me to discharge honourably the burdens of the great wealth which has flowed to me, and that keeps flowing in an ever-rising tide, from the Texas soil. There are not many dedicated persons in this shabby old world, and Crawford Hoolihan is one of them. Ireland may yet salute her, with holy Saint Brigid and Queen Maeve and the other great ladies of our storied past, not forgetting Graunya Wayl. I thank God humbly that she is far away from the hurly-burly and prairie stink of Texas oil, for nobody can pretend that gasoline is a pretty thing. And listen, Tim—don't be fooled if it seems for the present that she doesn't care a damn about you and takes you just for a gobshite of a caretaker. *I marked her card* and made it plump and plain that in my book you were the decentest and ablest young Irishman who ever wore a hat. I told her you were a sort of son of mine, though I didn't labour that point. Crawford doesn't wear her heart on her sleeve but she is far too shrewd to make any mistake about a man like you or even our mutual friend Sarsfield Slattery. Ah, how is Sarsfield? There is one little point I would like you to look to with your special care. Crawford has all the charity, humility and simplicity of a Saint Francis of Assisi or a Saint Teresa of Avila in her little finger but there is one thing she has yet to learn something about: I mean TACT. God help us but her honest direct attitude and methods might give offence to some of the over-sensitive slobs who still abound in Ireland's green and pleasant land. There is, if you like, something of the Saint Joan about her. Give her some help and guidance there, Tim! Never tire telling her that the Irish are easy-going (you and I know that they are just bone-lazy) and that it is far easier to lead them gently than to push them. I need hardly tell you that she has plenty of the proper contacts in high places, and I had Senator Hovis Oxter introduce her to old Mrs. Scheisemacher, mother of the American Ambassador in Dublin, Charlie Bendix Scheisemacher. I might tell you under the hat that Charlie is a stockholder and not a tiny one either in my H.P. Petroleum outfit and I can pull his whiskers any time I want to. You will find that Crawford will move fast as soon as she gets her bearings and if she has told you that she has already arranged to ship sago to Ireland in tankers as a stop-gap measure, it is perfectly true because she arranged it all through my own tanker subsidiary. I'm telling you, she'll wake Ireland up—and about time!

Do write to me, Tim, and tell me what is going on and how things are shaping. What impression has Crawford made on my native sod? How many local people has she met? What does Sarsfield Slattery think of her? And my old sparring partner Baggeley, how is he behaving and has he yet heard any tidings of my wife? My hope is that they won't meet, because the Doctor's health habits make him rather unreliable. The enclosed little extra cheque, which you need not mention to Crawford, is for yourself. Write, write, WRITE, Tim, and give me all the news.

Yours ever—Ned.

[The original typescript ends here.]

Appendices

Appendix I
[For] Ireland Home & Beauty (1940)

by Brian O’Nolan / Flann O’Brien [both names are listed in the original typescript] [1]

In my many walks with Mr. Cullen I had become accustomed to his habit of saluting the most unlikely people and explaining to me afterwards that they were in “the movement” and had been “mainly~~”~~ responsible[”] for such and such a piece of work when the fight against the British was at its hottest. He had never dwelt at any length on his own part in “the movement” beyond an occasional mention in passing that he had been present at the Howth Gun-running. For many years I had regarded this simple claim as [~~a delicate and not unmoving piece of modesty, clearly proving~~] [clear proof] that that daring bid to land the guns under the very noses of the British had been conceived by him alone and carried out practically single-handed. Later, when I learnt that he had been living in Howth during these eventful times and for many years before, I found several rather shabby thoughts [~~crowding~~] [coming] into my [~~brain~~] [head] every time [~~the burly form of my friend appeared on my horizon~~] [I met the good-natured burly patriot].

On the day I want to write about we were moving down the quays in the direction of Murtagh’s back-parlour. Mr. Cullen had been speaking when he suddenly stopped, nudged me and nodded ahead. Approaching us was a slender young man of twenty-two or so, dressed with great correctness in a dark suit. [His head was high.] He carried a cane and walked gracefully [~~carrying a high head.~~] [, and seemed to infect the whole street with his own distinction].

Mr. Cullen spoke when we were about to pass.

“How is Mr. Hogan?” he called.

---

[1] Editors’ Note: This previously unpublished typescript is an early draft version of “The Martyr’s Crown” (1950): Brian O’Nolan / Flann O’Brien, “[For] Ireland Home and Beauty” (1940), Series 2: Manuscripts, Box 4, Folder 10, Brian O’Nolan papers, Special Collections Research Center, Morris Library, Southern Illinois University, Carbondale. The twelve-page typescript contains some handwritten emendations by O’Nolan. The typed words which he crossed out in pen are reproduced in square brackets with a line through them [~~like so~~]; his handwritten emendations are reproduced in square brackets [like so]; illegible words are marked as [???]; [*//*] denotes a deleted paragraph break.

Instead of answering, the young man looked at Mr. Cullen [~~for the briefest possible interval of time with the most supercilious eye I have ever seen~~]. [It was a very brief look and his eye seemed supercilious]. It was not a look of scorn or derision or hatred. It seemed to say merely that Mr. Cullen was an unfamiliar thing and that his salutation was incomprehensible.

Mr. Cullen glanced at me and shook his head sadly.

"What does that mean?" I asked [him].

"I will tell you [all about it]," he said. "His mother was in the movement."

We had reached Murtagh's. Mr. Cullen led the way in with quiet efficiency and ordered two schooners. Mr. Murtagh himself was present and bade us the time of day. He was a massive bald man with a serious face and leaned far across the counter sideways on the pivot of his left arm, gesturing with his right and swiping idly at the flies.

"Well, Martin," he said.

"It is very close," said Mr. Cullen.

He drank deeply [~~from his pint~~]. The two of them gazed abstractedly at the counter [~~but I could see that their minds were completely blank~~] [as if nestling contentedly in each other's friendship]. [~~Idly~~] [The [???] had dragged] Mr. Murtagh['s] [trousers tight about the crotch. He adjusted himself carefully. I drank quietly for a while until I thought it would not be sacrilegious to break the silence. Then I said:]

"Who was our friend with the walking-stick?"

"Him?" said Mr. Cullen.

"Who is this, Martin?" asked Mr. Murtagh.

"O a very important gentleman."

"[And] Who is he when he is at home?" asked Mr. Murtagh.

"His name is Hogan," said Mr. Cullen. "I knew [~~her~~] [his mamma] well and [I] knew him, too. And when I met him five minutes ago in the street and gave him the time of day, he presented me with a look very few men would throw to a dog. 'Who the hell are you[?] [~~, if you understand me.~~] [Who the bloody hell are you to say good-day to me?] How would you like that, Ned? A man that was old enough to be his father."

"The word for that, Martin,["] [said Mr. Murtagh] is bad manners," [~~said Mr. Murtagh~~]. It is not a nice thing at all."

"[~~It is not~~] [Certainly I will say it is not what I would expect from him]," Mr. Cullen agreed, drinking heavily.

Mr. Murtagh slid his right hand [meditatively] along [a] [~~his~~] thigh.

"Hogan?" he said slowly. "Surely not the Harold's Cross crowd?"

"Not at all," said Mr. Cullen.

"Hogan?" said Mr. Murtagh. He frowned very darkly, weighing the word carefully in his mind. He seemed to be holding it up against every light that was in his memory. Suddenly he disengaged himself from the counter and went away to pull a bottle of stout for a customer at a distant part of the premises. Mr. Cullen turned to me.

"Hogan's mother," he said, "was one of the best. Ireland never had a better daughter. It was Ireland or nothing. There's a well-known saying about touching nothing that she did not adorn. [Well] She was one lady that filled the bill. It made you proud you were an Irishman."

"I suppose she did great work?"

"Great work?"

As if appalled by the limitations of human speech, he turned to his drink and finished it. Mr. Murtagh had returned and resumed his [attitude of] sidelong attention.

"By God I can't place that particular Hogan high or low," he said.

"As a matter of fact," said Mr. Cullen quickly, "his name isn't Hogan at all!"

"What?"

"A fact."

"Well Holy God, Martin," said Mr. Murtagh looking with mock anger at both of us, "what class of talk is that to be giving out?"

"Fill these glasses again," I said.

"What sort of a story is that?" he asked again, moving away to draw the porter.

Mr. Cullen smiled. He was the centre of mystery and was pleased with his importance.

"Now, Martin, fair is fair," said Mr. Murtagh, bringing up the drinks. He took my money absently in his right hand and fell into the side[w]ays [~~attitude~~] [stance] again.

"I will tell you the story," said Mr. Cullen. "Do you remember the Camden Street affair?"

"Which affair was that?" I asked.

"The famous ambush—Lord save us, surely you remember the day we lost Paddy Carroll the Lord have mercy on him. It was a party of military in three lorries. Paddy Carroll was in charge. The boys were in doorways and hanging out of the windows of tenement houses. There was holy bloody murder. If Paddy lost his life the other side paid a stiff price for it. There were more dead men in Camden Street that day than I ever laid my eyes on in my life. I happened to be present on the historic occasion."

I found myself wondering whether he had been living in Camden Street at the time. Looking into his earnest face as it looked brightly at the two of us, I felt ashamed of myself.

"It was a desperate piece of work. It was the most unmerciful shooting-match I ever witnessed."

He drank to fortify his mind.

"They rose in dark and evil days," said Mr. Murtagh, nodding.

"The next day," said Mr. Cullen, "the fun started in earnest. There were comb-outs and house-to-house searches. Every second man you met was a policeman or a soldier or a black-and-tan. They were like maggots under a stone. Thousands of people were arrested and most of them were given an unmerciful beating free of charge to show there was no ill-feeling.

"They were dark days," said Mr. Murtagh [gloomily].

[I knew that Mr. Cullen's superior grasp of tactics had brought him safely through all harm but I asked the question lightly as if I did not know the answer.]

"Did they get you?" I asked.

Mr. Cullen shook his head solemnly.

"They did not sir. And that's what I'm coming to. Myself and four of the boys were lying low. We knew what was good for us. It was Mick Hennessy that brought us to Mrs. Hogan's. She had a big house in Sandymount at the time. We had the run of the place, with first-class beds and the best to eat. I made out afterwards that it would cost you a pound a day for the same treatment at a good hotel."

"Tell me this," said Mr. Murtagh. [He looked as if some thought of considerable importance had suddenly lit upon his brain.] "Was there any husband there at all or what sort was this lady if you get my meaning?"

Mr. Cullen's face clouded.

"O Lord save us nothing like that," he said seriously, "nothing like that at all. O God no. She had any amount of cushions and curtains about the place that she had made herself. A most respectable woman. She had a husband alright but where he was I couldn't tell you. Every night we had prayers together in the kitchen."

"I see," said Mr. Murtagh. His interest in the story seemed [~~diminished~~] [to fade].

"We were there for three days. Most of us were feeling the want of exercise and we were [~~all~~] sick [and tired] playing draughts. At about five o'clock in the evening of the fourth day when we were all in the drawing-room reading the papers and yarning, we heard cars drawing up in the street below. I needn't tell you that we knew the sound of the old Crossleys by heart."

"I see," said Mr. Murtagh. "A raid?"

"Hennessy went over to the window and peeped out. When he turned round, his face was the colour of that, look."

Mr. Cullen put a finger on a white water-jug [, with his nail tapping it].

"As pale as a ghost," he added, looking in turn at each of us. [*#*] "'What's up, Mick?' I asked. 'Two lorries of military,' said Mick."

"Well God knows," said Mr. Murtagh, "I'd rather be here than there that day."

Mr. Cullen again looked to each of us.

"I stood up with the 'Irish Times' in my hand," he said, "and did two minutes worth of very hard thinking. I took the situation in at a glance. Unless something drastic was done and done quickly, we were all bitched. Downstairs the hall-door was being hammered till the house shook."

"A delicate situation," I interposed.

"There was one chance. I took charge immediately. I put up my hand for silence [~~and spoke quickly~~] [although there was plenty of it there without being asked for]. 'Listen,' I said, 'we're in a tight corner but there's one chance if we keep our heads. *This is a kip,*' says I, '*and you,*' says I to Mrs. Hogan, '*you're in charge of it. We're all respectable married men having an evening out.*'"

Mr. Murtagh smiled and wiped the counter with round meditative swipes.

"Well I wouldn't doubt you, Martin," he said. "If you have to think of a story at all, you'll think of a good one. How did our ladyship take the news?"

Mr. Cullen put his finger again on the water-jug.

"[First] She went the colour of that [~~first~~], [look]" he said, "and then she went as red as a turkey-cock. I think she lost the power of speech. Only temporarily, of course. We all stood there looking at her [like a lot of dumb clucks]."

"A delicate situation," I put in again.

"Delicate? You could [~~nearly~~] hear the hair growing on your head. Poor Mrs. Hogan—you could see her telling herself that it would have to be done for Ireland and then finding it hard to believe what she had told herself. And all the time the hammering that was going on downstairs would put the fear of God in you."

"Of course," said Mr. Murtagh [~~delicately~~] [finely], "if the intention was pure and no pleasure was taken, there would be no question of mortal sin."

"Is that so?" said Mr. Cullen.

"I think that is the official Church view."

"I see. Well, to make a long story short, my bold woman marches down the stairs and throws open the door. I sneaked down to the landing to hear what was [~~said~~] [going on]. I could hear two voices—high-class officers' voices, you know—asking her were there any men in the house and no question of please or thank-you. I nearly dropped dead when I heard her answering them. She took off the accent of a fish-woman to a T. She said there were a few men in the house certainly[.][~~—w~~][W]hy wouldn't there be[?] She was sniggering and using plenty of personality with the two officers."

"Well dear knows," said Mr. Murtagh, smiling [as if against his will].

"One of the officers gave a bit of a laugh and said something about human nature and then I heard the other gentleman speaking in a low voice and there were several more laughs, some of them from Mrs. Hogan. This went on for five minutes. Then I heard the two boyos coming into the house and going into a room off the hall. They were inside for twenty minutes and then they came out and went away."

"By God there's a story there somewhere," said Mr. Murtagh warmly. "If you wrote down the inside story of what happened there you would make a fortune in America. Did you ever read a book called 'Ten Nights of Life and Love' by Charles Paris?"

"I did not," said Mr. Cullen.

"Well by God that was the business," said Mr. Murtagh.

"Is that the end of the story about Mrs. Hogan?" I inquired.

"It's the end of that story," said Mr. Cullen, "but there was what is called a sequel. At the end of a certain length of time there was a question of a baby. It was kept very dark, of course, and a yarn was put out about an orphan arriving from the country. The new arrival got the name of Hogan and it was this same particular young gentleman that cut the nose off me in the street not half an hour ago. What do you think of that?"

Mr. Murtagh shook his head and smiled.

"It would be the mercy of Providence," he said, "if somebody told that proud Irish gentleman who his two fathers were. Eh, Ned?" [He laughed hollowly.]

"And why is he so proud?" I asked, "why does he walk as if he[r] owned the earth? [Why did he not answer when you saluted?]"

"Do you not see it?" cried Mr. Cullen. "Thousands and thousands of men have died for Ireland. Some of them have been hanged, some shot and some of them were roasted. The men of Ninety-Eight were strapped [with their face out] to the wheels of carts and flogged on the belly till their bowels came right out of them. That was a nice cup of tea to drink for Ireland. They were all good patriots [, good [???] are rare]."

"I see that," said Mr. Murtagh.

"But Hogan wasn't one of that crowd. *He* was *born* for Ireland!"

He looked to each of us in triumph, finished his drink swiftly and walked to the door, waving his farewell with one hand and wiping his mouth with the back of the other.

"Die-for-Ireland how are you," he called. [END][2]

Mr. Murtagh wiped his counter carefully [and then looked down at it for a while].

"Well Holy God," he said [to me] at last, "if you wrote that story down you would make a queer penny from American copyrights. 'The Man That Was Born For Ireland,' eh? By God whether it's good or bad it's new. Or 'The Woman That Sinned To Save Her Country's Wrong.' She was a queer woman, there is no doubt about it. Not that it is for you or me to sit in judgment, of course. Holy God Almighty."

"To the pure all things are pure," I muttered.

"That is the official Church view, of course. But Lord save us, the poor unfortunate son must have been a queer cranky article. What did he look like?"

"O he looked the same as you or me," I said.

I left Mr. Murtagh soon after for I did not wish to be pressed for the young man's description. This was because I knew the young man. [~~He was extremely short-sighted.~~] [He was neither supercilious nor shy merely short-sighted]. He was studying for the priesthood in Rome and was evidently home on [~~leave~~] [holiday]. [~~His second name was Murtagh.~~] [He was Mr. Murtagh's second son.] [I left the shop and went away, preoccupied with the strange personality of my friend Mr. Cullen.]

[2] Editors' Note: All the remaining lines after O'Nolan's handwritten note 'END' have been lightly crossed out in pen.

Appendix II

EDITORS' NOTE: As indicated in our Introduction, we include the following story, "Naval Control," first published when O'Brien was just twenty-one years old, as a speculative gesture designed to generate further discussion and discovery. Such a gesture ultimately requires a full critical examination, but some initial rationale for including a hitherto unknown pen name and story is briefly offered here.

The story was first brought to our attention by Jack Fennell, who as well as being a fine translator of Gaelic texts is also a leading authority on Irish science fiction. Jack noted how Everett F. Bleiler, in his exhaustive bibliography of every pulp science fiction story published by Hugo Gernsback from 1926 to 1936, includes a reference to a short story by a mysterious "John Shamus O'Donnell." Unfortunately, while Bleiler has biographies for almost every other author in his index, no information is provided for O'Donnell. "John Shamus," whoever he was, does not seem to have published anything else. Bleiler's description, synopsis, and rather blithe critical judgment of "Naval Control" runs as follows:

> Short-short story.
> *Place*: the San Francisco area.
> The narrator, who seems to have been a missionary, laments the death of his wife Florence Minerva, who, he says, clad half the natives of Peru in Mother Hubbards and converted them as Baptists. But his friend the renowned Irish scientist Egan will construct for him an android that is the exact image of Florence Minerva.
>
> Florence Minerva the Second, who is operated by electricity, is all she should be in appearance, but there are behavioral problems. Atmospheric electricity sets her off; sitting on an iron bench drains her magnetism; and proximity to a certain sailor with a silver plate in his head induces telepathic communication (singing ribald sailor songs) and erotic feelings. At the last, as the sailor ships out to sea, Florence Minerva the Second wades out into the water after him and is lost.

Amateurish, but occasionally amusing.[1]

To date, no archival material has been found to verify the story's provenance. Electronic concordancing and corpus linguistics may be of some value here, but we leave that investigation for another time. For the moment, though, we would just like to point out a few basic elements in the story which, for us, mark it out as the work of Flann O'Brien.

First, there is the thematic fascination with trains, doubles, and strange names, all reminiscent of stories such as "John Duffy's Brother" and "Donabate" as well as novels like *The Third Policeman* and *At Swim-Two-Birds*. Second, there is the typically playful use of the epistolary mode, where letters serve to splinter the text into multiple voices (something that O'Brien uses to great effect elsewhere). Third, the parodic use of science—or science reformulated as farce—is particularly characteristic of O'Brien. Note, for instance, the comic consequences of the mechanical Florence Minerva's wiring malfunctions and the mock-serious tone of the pseudo-scientific jargon, as in the description of the the electrical sympathy between her "fissures and sulci" and the "silver-pated" sailor. (A rather misogynistic view of women is another, less attractive, O'Brien characteristic.) Fourth, the family resemblance between the mad Irish scientist Professor J. Egan and one of O'Brien's great creations, the idiot savant de Selby, is striking, even if Egan is a less refined version. Fifth, and while the Irishness of the Professor is noteworthy, even more striking is the pen name "John Shamus O'Donnell," which seems to prefigure the parodic name "Jams O'Donnell" in *The Poor Mouth* (Jams and Shamus are derived from the same name, James). Sixth, and more speculatively, perhaps, much of "Naval Control" is based in "Beal Gulch," California—a variation, possibly, on Bear Gulch Road in Oakland, California—although the word "Béal" is also the Gaelic for mouth.

Throughout "Naval Control," significant intertextual and intratextual connections with other O'Brien works are also evident. For

[1] Everett F. Bleiler, with Richard J. Bleiler, *Science-Fiction: The Gernsback Years: A Complete Coverage of the Genre Magazines 'Amazing', 'Astounding', 'Wonder', and Others from 1926 through 1936* (Kent, Ohio; London: Kent State UP, 1998), p. 311 (entry 1076).

example, at one point we are told that Florence "burst forth in a ribald sailor's song, which would have been proper in a Singapore drinking dive," echoing a phrase used in *The Third Policeman*, in relation to Policeman MacCruiskeen's chest: "It was a brown chest like those owned by seafaring men or lascars from Singapore." (Eagle-eyed readers will already have noted that Singapore is mentioned twice in *Slattery's Sago Saga*.)

A much more compelling connection, though, lies in the closure to the story: "With the spiritual poise of a Lady of the Lake walking towards her Jurgen, she walked toward the ship and the sunset, till, through my tears, I saw her sun-bonnet disappear beneath the waves!" This slightly elliptical denouement mirrors the enigmatic ending of "John Duffy's Brother," with its resonant—but unspecified—allusion to John Keats's sonnet, "On First Looking into Chapman's Homer" (1816): "Never once did the strange malady return. But to this day John Duffy's brother starts at the rumble of a train in the Liffey tunnel and stands rooted to the road when he comes suddenly on a level-crossing—silent, so to speak, upon a peak in Darien."[2] More specifically, the intertextual invocation at the end of "Naval Control" is to James Branch Cabell's *Jurgen: A Comedy of Justice* (1919), in which the eponymous hero counts among his amorous conquests a mysterious "Lady of the Lake." (Our Lady of the Lake is also mentioned, of course, in *Slattery's Sago Saga*.) As various scholars have pointed out, Cabell's novels were an acknowledged influence on *At Swim-Two-Birds*, or as Anthony Cronin has noted:

> The novel within a novel had been used by at least two authors whose books Brian O'Nolan had read. One of these was the now almost forgotten American, James Branch Cabell, whose novels, *Jurgen* and *The Cream of the Jest*, had been passed from hand to hand among O'Nolan's contemporaries at UCD and who was subsequently to be

[2] For a detailed discussion of this intertextual strategy, see Keith Hopper, "Coming Off the Rails: The Strange Case of 'John Duffy's Brother,'" *Flann O'Brien: Contesting Legacies*, ed. Werner Huber, Paul Fagan, and Ruben Borg (Cork: Cork UP, forthcoming).

referred to as James Joyce Cabell in "Cruiskeen Lawn".[3]

Overall, and while we think this makes a compelling case for O'Brien's authorship, we leave that final judgment to others. In the meantime, here's the story: enjoy!

> *Why, some of our readers have asked, do we take science fiction so seriously? Is there no humor in it? We think there is. But we want to hear from more of our readers about this story, which we are using as an experiment. We think it is very ingenious and cleverly worked out.*
>
> —Original Headnote to "Naval Control," *Amazing Stories Quarterly*, 1932[4]

With the spiritual poise of a Lady of the Lake walking toward her Jurgen, she walked toward the ship and the sunset. . . .

Naval Control

By John Shamus O'Donnell

I AM in a saddened and unbearable state of melancholia. Four months ago today my Florence Minerva succumbed to the deadly fever of a South American jungle.

What a woman! I will never find another like her; she was the perfect helpmate. When I would be weary while working on my mining invention, she would spur me on with intensive spiritual quotations, and not only to me was she an inspiration.

To the natives she was a blessing. I firmly believe if she had lived another ten years she would have accomplished the full attire of at least half the female native population of Peru.

I remember now, as when we first arrived, looking about with a Napoleonic glint through her glasses at the shameless half nude natives, how she struggled to moralize them in the early stages. She would no sooner get a native woman to drape herself more heavily, than one of the burly bucks would take it away from her, promenading through the village street with her drapings.

Overcoming all these obstacles, she had the village going Baptist with glorious hallelujahs, when she was stricken by fever, and we laid away my spiritual six foot Jeanne d'Arc.

I drifted back to my laboratory house at Beal Gulch outside of Oakland, California, on the Golden Gate, where I gaze at the fog-filtered sunsets and think with pensive sadness of my Florence Minerva.

I've tried the subterfuge of housekeepers and servants but they all seem such strangers in

WHY, some of our readers have asked, do we take science fiction so seriously? Is there no humor in it? We think there is. But we want to hear from more of our readers about this story, which we are using as an experiment. We think it is very ingenious and cleverly worked out.

141

[3] Anthony Cronin, *No Laughing Matter: The Life and Times of Flann O'Brien* (London: Grafton, 1989), p. 83. See also Anne Clissmann, *Flann O'Brien: A Critical Introduction to his Writings* (Dublin: Gill & Macmillan, 1975), p. 93.

[4] John Shamus O'Donnell, "Naval Control," *Amazing Stories Quarterly* [USA] 5.1 (Winter 1932), pp. 141–43.

Naval Control (1932)
by John Shamus O'Donnell

I am in a saddened and unbearable state of melancholia. Four months ago today my Florence Minerva succumbed to the deadly fever of a South American jungle.

What a woman! I will never find another like her; she was the perfect helpmate. When I would be weary while working on my mining invention, she would spur me on with intensive spiritual quotations, and not only to me was she an inspiration.

To the natives she was a blessing. I firmly believe if she had lived another ten years she would have accomplished the full attire of at least half the female native population of Peru.

I remember now, as when we first arrived, looking about with a Napoleonic glint through her glasses at the shameless half nude natives, how she struggled to moralize them in the early stages. She would no sooner get a native woman to drape herself more heavily, than one of the burly bucks would take it away from her, promenading through the village street with her drapings.

Overcoming all these obstacles, she had the village going Baptist with glorious hallelujahs, when she was stricken by fever, and we laid away my spiritual six-foot Jeanne d'Arc.

I drifted back to my laboratory home at Beal Gulch outside of Oakland, California, on the Golden Gate, where I gaze at the fog-filtered sunsets and think with pensive sadness of my Florence Minerva.

I've tried the subterfuge of housekeepers and servants but they all seem such strangers in the house that Florence Minerva enveloped with her personality.

Once again I go to my lonely bed torturing myself with a look at one of Florence Minerva's night caps, which still hang under our favourite epigram, "Love, pure and unadulterated."

Today I received a gleam of insane hope through my old colleague, Professor Egan, the Irish scientist.

It seems, after twenty years of constant labour, that he has at last perfected his mechanical human, controlled by his advanced inventions on power transmissions, and on account of the devotion held for my dear wife and me, he has collaborated with a modernistic plastic surgeon, and a marvellous sculptor, producing, he says, an almost human likeness of the departed Florence Minerva. In his letter he expresses the desire to have his invention in my laboratory home, where we both could experiment and, perhaps, improve on her life-like qualities and where he would be unhampered for space or bothered by curiosity seekers.

I immediately wired my acquiescence and waited with feverish impatience.

He answered immediately and said that he would make the daring experiment of bringing her out on the train intact as his travelling companion; and would start as soon as he could pack his laboratory instruments and spare parts for Florence Minerva.

Six days later I received a wire announcing his departure in this manner—"Taxied to the Grand Central Station with Florence Minerva, and left New York quite successfully. So far she is human, all too human, even attracting a bold smile from a sailor loafing in the station."

The next communication I received was this, by Western Union—"March 17, Garrison, N.Y., Safely seated in Pullman, just one minor accident so far; on boarding train, one of the radio transfusion wires in my vest became shorted and Florence Minerva fell through the glass in the Pullman window; in my momentary excitement I seized her by the throat and sat her down; naturally she tried to repeat the gesture but I finally managed to straighten the wires and she dropped back into normalcy. I greatly fear this has caused undesirable comment; I hear loud indignant buzzings made by two rather spinsterish looking old ladies seated in back of us, who seem to think Florence Minerva was either trying to commit suicide or make an escape. I had Florence Minerva turn about and explain, in her maidenly way, that she was subject to fainting spells and not to be alarmed. I seem to have the situation well in hand again and will keep in touch with you constantly. Signed, J. Egan."

The next I heard was this: "Aboard the Mohawk Limited, 9 A.M., the last twelve hours have been most hectic. I fear the two old ladies are liable to cause serious complications, they watch us most sharply. Florence Minerva and I retired to our berths at ten P.M. I thought it wiser that we sleep with our clothes on as I am in deadly fear of getting her wires crossed again. This was poor foresight for I overlooked the disreputable condition we were bound to have when we arose in the morning. We arose early hoping to escape the congestion one always finds in Pullman wash-rooms, also the two spinsters, but, alas, they were already up and their curiosity hadn't abated over night; they eyed us sharply and noted our rumpled condition suspiciously. I made a lightning-like peep of the ladies' washroom and found it untenanted. I then sent Florence Minerva in and in a few moments brought her out again. I had her essay a good morning to the old ladies who replied quite stiffly, 'Dear me, I'll be glad when this trip is over!' Florence Minerva has developed an off-key in her cerebral cortex—when one of the old ladies asked her if she happened to be a Methodist, she shouted, with the gusto of a longshoreman, that she was a hot shot three o'clock blonde when, according to my A B C D wiring for the larynx, tongue and throat, she should have answered with a cultured, 'No, Baptist.' This, I am afraid has created another unpleasant scene, the conductor even coming up to inquire if anything were wrong. I soothed things as much as possible, by explaining that my wife was subject to a form of nervous insanity if anything of a religious nature was mentioned. Things are resuming normalcy again, thank God! Will wire you again shortly. Signed, J. Egan."

"Mohawk Limited, 18th. A terrible thing has happened. I find Florence Minerva reacts uncontrollably to heat lightning. Everything was quite peaceable, when about noon, there arose a burst of heat lightning. Florence Minerva nearly startled me out of my senses when she burst forth in a ribald sailor's song, which would have been proper in a Singapore drinking dive but it was terrible in a Pullman. This was evidently a thought transfusion from the sailor in the Grand Central Station. I shorted her motor-nerve battery, but the damage was already done. The old ladies shrieked, rude men guffawed; we were in wild confusion. Immediately I had Florence Minerva faint, then attempted to explain in an incoherent way that she was having another one of her spells; the conductor growled that if she had any more we would be left, bag and baggage, at the next water tank. It seems every eye is on us, I am praying for night to come, as it's just about time to recharge her batteries."

"Nineteenth, Mohawk Limited, a mystifying thing is happening. I find the sailor who smiled at Florence Minerva in the Grand Central Station is aboard the train. When he walks by our seat, she buzzes and shakes in a disconcerting way; I short circuit her every time. I cannot seem to understand this. Perplexedly yours, J. Egan."

"Nineteenth, one P.M., Mohawk Limited, Amazing! I had a searching conversation with the sailor and I find the cause of Florence Minerva's sympathetic disorders. It seems that during the war he had an accident which resulted in a silver plate being placed in his head near his brain; therefore with the fissures and sulci of Florence Minerva's brain being silver, there seems to be an electrical sympathy between the two convolutions; I sincerely hope nothing comes of this. Incidentally, he's going to San Francisco also. J. Egan."

"Twentieth, 10 A.M., Mohawk Limited, Florence Minerva behaving in an excellent way, sailor confining himself in smoking room. I will arrive Oakland Mole tomorrow at eleven A.M. Approximately. J. Egan."

Ah! The momentous day is here! Can't you picture my excitement? Today I will meet the reincarnation of my dear departed wife. I wonder, can it be possible she will appear as life-like and real as the doctor has stated; it must be so for no one has guessed the secret on the train.

I dressed today as if I were starting on the second honeymoon, arrived at the Oakland Mole in the same frame of mind as if I were waiting for Florence Minerva to step out of the vault. I wondered how accurately they had copied her features and form. Well, we shall see soon, now, as I hear the train clanging in. There he is, and oh, can it be possible! I feel dizzy—it must be some Hindoo magic, for I see my dear wife in person towering above the crowd and swinging towards me with a timid smile of welcome. I must be going crazy. But no, there is my dear old friend, Dr. Egan, labouring towards me with his ponderous bags.

I am trembling and so overcome with an unexplainable shyness, I hardly know how to greet Florence Minerva and the doctor. But finally we are through this ordeal and seated in my car, where I have a chance to look over Florence Minerva and Dr. Egan, who seems to have, I might say, a more sophisticated and worldly appearance but, still apparently, the same dynamic energy. We are now nearing Beal Gulch where I await with pride the joy of showing Florence Minerva and the doctor the magnificent laboratories I have installed for us three, overlooking the Golden Gate.

Florence Minerva and the doctor seem delighted in their new home. There seems to be just one rift in the scientific calm. I fear Dr. Egan is slightly inclined toward sentimentalism. I notice him, in unguarded moments, gazing with tender devotion towards Florence Minerva. This has created a difficult problem for me, for even though Dr. Egan has created Florence Minerva, I feel that she is mine by every spiritual right. I am afraid it is rather straining our friendship. This morning we were even a bit rude over her. The doctor, in the final work of Florence Minerva's brain control, made a grave error. Instead of the simple sweetness of Florence Minerva Number One, she seems to have a suppressed eroticism, which I firmly believe will not coordinate with the mechanical organic system. I stated my belief to the doctor, also adding I thought it sacrilegious to the memory of Florence Minerva Number One; he had the audacity to reply, that perhaps Florence Minerva Number One had been that way, I having the usual intelligence of genus husband.

But we must forget our household squabbles, and now combat mutually a new scientific hazard that has appeared on the horizon. It seems this silver-pated sailor has arrived on the scene again, being stationed at Vallejo, not far from our home, the doctor having seen him while on a trip to town with Florence Minerva. The meeting was unavoidable and Florence Minerva was, as usual, uncontrollable, making herself a perfect mechanical idiot by greeting him as if she were Minnie the mermaid greeting the long-lost boatswain of a whaler. This was extremely humiliating, as you may imagine, to a dignified old gentleman such as our Dr. Egan. We pondered over this new difficulty and the only solution we could see was keeping Florence Minerva away from the Naval Station and confining her on the sailor's liberty days. We also had a solution of the difficulty in the fact that the sailor's ship was being sent to sea shortly.

Life hummed along in a happy orgy of detecting and eradicating flaws in Florence Minerva and adding more complexity to her brain mechanism. We, of course, have Florence Minerva's orthodox habits dialed quite expertly, but we find in our eagerness to improve, we must have merged some wires, which have produced unchartable complexes; we are watching her closely, and expect, by working her in the usual lanes such as her household duties and church, these wires will work back in place again.

Today was quite a domestic little scene about the laboratory. We were going over her wiring, checking batteries, polishing nails, taking the shine off the nose, washing the hair and deciding which dresses she should wear for the week, quite a problem, I assure you, for two middle-aged gentlemen. Here again the doctor and I were at sword's points, he being inclined towards an English walking suit while I approved of a dignified Mother Hubbard, but we compromised on a gay middy-blouse and sun-bonnet, very charming, I pledge my word.

Today being Sunday, we went to church where we made another momentous but disconcerting discovery. There is a distinct reverberation in Florence Minerva's system to organ music. We were sitting quietly listening to the sweet strains of "Over the River," when Florence Minerva emitted a protracted dog-like howl which stopped the organ but started everything else. The simple country folk, thinking she was beset by devils, broke into loud praying, led by the minister. In this passion of theological fervour we made our escape with Florence Minerva between us.

As much as I enjoy the walks to town with Florence Minerva, I am afraid I shall have to discontinue them; they are too risky. Today, on arriving in town, it being a sunny day, I left her sitting on the bench in front of the store while I made the purchases. On returning, I discovered I had made a very stupid blunder. I had left her sitting on this bench which, being iron, had drained a large part of her magnetism. We started for home immediately but she staggered most erratically, giving the appearance of being in a most inebriated condition. We were followed at our heels by small boys and the village loafers who used this scene to indulge in vulgar witticisms such as, "Don't walk home, lady; the old stiff got you drunk, make him drag you home!" With Florence Minerva at last becoming so weak, and the jeers of the crowd becoming so obnoxious, I threw her six feet of pulchritude over my shoulder and broke into a mad gallop. Outdistancing my pursuers, I arrived home red-faced and my heart palpitating most dangerously.

Life is but a bridge; pass over but build not a house thereon. I have been sacrificed on the altar of Love in a most hideous way; the fires of my love for Florence Minerva Number One had only been allowed to cool slightly when Florence Minerva Number Two arrived to give me all my old love again, plus the scientific love. Now I am robbed of everything!

We had sent Florence Minerva for her usual morning walk on our private beach, thinking she was quite safe. What fools we were! We had overlooked the navy!

The cursed silver-pated sailor had been called to sea and, as his ship headed out the Golden Gate, that fatal magnetism caught our Florence Minerva. Standing at the other end of the beach, I saw, too late, what had happened. I pressed the controls in vain! With the spiritual poise of a Lady of the Lake walking toward her Jurgen, she walked toward the ship and the sunset, till, through my tears, I saw her sun-bonnet disappear beneath the waves!

Contributors

Neil Murphy teaches at NTU, Singapore. He is the author of *Irish Fiction and Postmodern Doubt* (2004) and editor of *Aidan Higgins: The Fragility of Form* (2009). He co-edited (with Keith Hopper) the special Flann O'Brien centenary issue of the *Review of Contemporary Fiction* (2011), and has published articles and book chapters on contemporary fiction, Irish writing, and theories of reading.

Keith Hopper teaches Literature and Film Studies at Oxford University's Department for Continuing Education, and is a Research Fellow in the Centre for Irish Studies at St Mary's University College, Twickenham. He is the author of *Flann O'Brien: A Portrait of the Artist as a Young Post-modernist* (revised edition 2009); general editor of the twelve-volume *Ireland into Film* series (2001–7); and co-editor (with Neil Murphy and Ondřej Pilný) of a special "Neglected Irish Fiction" issue of *Litteraria Pragensia* (2013). He is a regular contributor to the *Times Literary Supplement.*

Jack Fennell is a researcher at the University of Limerick. His research interests are Irish literature, science fiction, and cultural studies. He has published essays on Irish dystopian literature, the aesthetics of comic-book justice, and the politics of monsters and monstrous communities, as well as contributing informal articles to *The James Joyce Literary Supplement* and the Flann O'Brien e-journal, *The Parish Review*. His doctoral thesis is on the subject of Irish science fiction, from the 1850s to the present day.

Eddie O'Kane is an artist and a Director of Cavanacor Gallery, Lifford, County Donegal, Ireland. He won the first prize for painting at the Oireachtas National Art Exhibition in Cork in 2008. His artwork features in many public and private collections in Ireland and abroad. From 1975 to 2009 he was a lecturer at Letterkenny Institute of Technology, Donegal. He was also the Institute's first Industrial Liaison Officer.

The painting featured on the cover of this book—"Flann O'Brien I" (50 x 40 cm, acrylic on canvas, 2011)—was first shown as part of a two-man exhibition of artwork by Eddie O'Kane and his son David O'Kane. The exhibition was entitled "I have looked everywhere that can be looked," which was held at Cavanacor Gallery in 2011 to commemorate the centenary of Brian O'Nolan's birth. The painting shows a view of the Bowling Green in Strabane from the window of the house where O'Nolan was born. The row of houses opposite is taken from a photograph from the early 1900s; the view has remained relatively unchanged up to the present day. A shadowy Flann O'Brien is included looking towards the window. To the right of the house was the town's Police Station (not shown).

Flann O'Brien, whose real name was Brian O'Nolan, also wrote under the pen name of Myles na Gopaleen. He was born in 1911 in County Tyrone. A resident of Dublin, he graduated from University College after a brilliant career as a student (editing a magazine called *Blather*) and joined the Civil Service, in which he eventually attained a senior position. He wrote throughout his life, which ended in Dublin on April 1, 1966. His other novels include *The Dalkey Archive*, *The Third Policeman*, *The Hard Life*, and *The Poor Mouth*, all available from Dalkey Archive Press. Also available are three volumes of his newspaper columns, as well as his *Plays and Teleplays*.

SELECTED DALKEY ARCHIVE TITLES

Michal Ajvaz, *The Golden Age.*
The Other City.
Pierre Albert-Birot, *Grabinoulor.*
Yuz Aleshkovsky, *Kangaroo.*
Felipe Alfau, *Chromos.*
Locos.
Ivan Ângelo, *The Celebration.*
The Tower of Glass.
António Lobo Antunes, *Knowledge of Hell.*
The Splendor of Portugal.
Alain Arias-Misson, *Theatre of Incest.*
John Ashbery and James Schuyler, *A Nest of Ninnies.*
Robert Ashley, *Perfect Lives.*
Gabriela Avigur-Rotem, *Heatwave and Crazy Birds.*
Djuna Barnes, *Ladies Almanack.*
Ryder.
John Barth, *LETTERS.*
Sabbatical.
Donald Barthelme, *The King.*
Paradise.
Svetislav Basara, *Chinese Letter.*
Miquel Bauçà, *The Siege in the Room.*
René Belletto, *Dying.*
Marek Bieńczyk, *Transparency.*
Andrei Bitov, *Pushkin House.*
Andrej Blatnik, *You Do Understand.*
Louis Paul Boon, *Chapel Road.*
My Little War.
Summer in Termuren.
Roger Boylan, *Killoyle.*
Ignácio de Loyola Brandão, *Anonymous Celebrity.*
Zero.
Bonnie Bremser, *Troia: Mexican Memoirs.*
Christine Brooke-Rose, *Amalgamemnon.*
Brigid Brophy, *In Transit.*
Gerald L. Bruns, *Modern Poetry and the Idea of Language.*
Gabrielle Burton, *Heartbreak Hotel.*
Michel Butor, *Degrees.*
Mobile.
G. Cabrera Infante, *Infante's Inferno.*
Three Trapped Tigers.
Julieta Campos, *The Fear of Losing Eurydice.*
Anne Carson, *Eros the Bittersweet.*
Orly Castel-Bloom, *Dolly City.*
Louis-Ferdinand Céline, *Castle to Castle.*
Conversations with Professor Y.
London Bridge.
Normance.
North.
Rigadoon.
Marie Chaix, *The Laurels of Lake Constance.*
Hugo Charteris, *The Tide Is Right.*
Eric Chevillard, *Demolishing Nisard.*
Marc Cholodenko, *Mordechai Schamz.*
Joshua Cohen, *Witz.*
Emily Holmes Coleman, *The Shutter of Snow.*
Robert Coover, *A Night at the Movies.*
Stanley Crawford, *Log of the S.S. The Mrs Unguentine.*
Some Instructions to My Wife.
René Crevel, *Putting My Foot in It.*
Ralph Cusack, *Cadenza.*
Nicholas Delbanco, *The Count of Concord.*
Sherbrookes.
Nigel Dennis, *Cards of Identity.*
Peter Dimock, *A Short Rhetoric for Leaving the Family.*
Ariel Dorfman, *Konfidenz.*
Coleman Dowell, *Island People.*
Too Much Flesh and Jabez.
Arkadii Dragomoshchenko, *Dust.*
Rikki Ducornet, *The Complete Butcher's Tales.*
The Fountains of Neptune.
The Jade Cabinet.
Phosphor in Dreamland.
William Eastlake, *The Bamboo Bed.*
Castle Keep.
Lyric of the Circle Heart.
Jean Echenoz, *Chopin's Move.*
Stanley Elkin, *A Bad Man.*
Criers and Kibitzers, Kibitzers and Criers.
The Dick Gibson Show.
The Franchiser.
The Living End.
Mrs. Ted Bliss.
François Emmanuel, *Invitation to a Voyage.*
Salvador Espriu, *Ariadne in the Grotesque Labyrinth.*
Leslie A. Fiedler, *Love and Death in the American Novel.*
Juan Filloy, *Op Oloop.*
Andy Fitch, *Pop Poetics.*
Gustave Flaubert, *Bouvard and Pécuchet.*
Kass Fleisher, *Talking out of School.*
Ford Madox Ford, *The March of Literature.*
Jon Fosse, *Aliss at the Fire.*
Melancholy.
Max Frisch, *I'm Not Stiller.*
Man in the Holocene.
Carlos Fuentes, *Christopher Unborn.*
Distant Relations.
Terra Nostra.
Where the Air Is Clear.
Takehiko Fukunaga, *Flowers of Grass.*
William Gaddis, *J R.*
The Recognitions.
Janice Galloway, *Foreign Parts.*
The Trick Is to Keep Breathing.
William H. Gass, *Cartesian Sonata and Other Novellas.*
Finding a Form.
A Temple of Texts.
The Tunnel.
Willie Masters' Lonesome Wife.
Gérard Gavarry, *Hoppla! 1 2 3.*
Etienne Gilson, *The Arts of the Beautiful.*
Forms and Substances in the Arts.
C. S. Giscombe, *Giscome Road.*
Here.
Douglas Glover, *Bad News of the Heart.*
Witold Gombrowicz, *A Kind of Testament.*
Paulo Emílio Sales Gomes, *P's Three Women.*
Georgi Gospodinov, *Natural Novel.*
Juan Goytisolo, *Count Julian.*
Juan the Landless.
Makbara.
Marks of Identity.

SELECTED DALKEY ARCHIVE TITLES

Henry Green, *Back.*
Blindness.
Concluding.
Doting.
Nothing.
Jack Green, *Fire the Bastards!*
Jiří Gruša, *The Questionnaire.*
Mela Hartwig, *Am I a Redundant Human Being?*
John Hawkes, *The Passion Artist.*
Whistlejacket.
Elizabeth Heighway, ed., *Contemporary Georgian Fiction.*
Aleksandar Hemon, ed., *Best European Fiction.*
Aidan Higgins, *Balcony of Europe.*
Blind Man's Bluff
Bornholm Night-Ferry.
Flotsam and Jetsam.
Langrishe, Go Down.
Scenes from a Receding Past.
Keizo Hino, *Isle of Dreams.*
Kazushi Hosaka, *Plainsong.*
Aldous Huxley, *Antic Hay.*
Crome Yellow.
Point Counter Point.
Those Barren Leaves.
Time Must Have a Stop.
Naoyuki Ii, *The Shadow of a Blue Cat.*
Gert Jonke, *The Distant Sound.*
Geometric Regional Novel.
Homage to Czerny.
The System of Vienna.
Jacques Jouet, *Mountain R.*
Savage.
Upstaged.
Mieko Kanai, *The Word Book.*
Yoram Kaniuk, *Life on Sandpaper.*
Hugh Kenner, *Flaubert.*
Joyce and Beckett: The Stoic Comedians.
Joyce's Voices.
Danilo Kiš, *The Attic.*
Garden, Ashes.
The Lute and the Scars
Psalm 44.
A Tomb for Boris Davidovich.
Anita Konkka, *A Fool's Paradise.*
George Konrád, *The City Builder.*
Tadeusz Konwicki, *A Minor Apocalypse.*
The Polish Complex.
Menis Koumandareas, *Koula.*
Elaine Kraf, *The Princess of 72nd Street.*
Jim Krusoe, *Iceland.*
Ayşe Kulin, *Farewell: A Mansion in Occupied Istanbul.*
Emilio Lascano Tegui, *On Elegance While Sleeping.*
Eric Laurrent, *Do Not Touch.*
Violette Leduc, *La Bâtarde.*
Edouard Levé, *Autoportrait.*
Suicide.
Mario Levi, *Istanbul Was a Fairy Tale.*
Deborah Levy, *Billy and Girl.*
José Lezama Lima, *Paradiso.*
Rosa Liksom, *Dark Paradise.*
Osman Lins, *Avalovara.*
The Queen of the Prisons of Greece.
Alf Mac Lochlainn, *The Corpus in the Library.*
Out of Focus.
Ron Loewinsohn, *Magnetic Field(s).*
Mina Loy, *Stories and Essays of Mina Loy.*
D. Keith Mano, *Take Five.*
Micheline Aharonian Marcom, *The Mirror in the Well.*
Ben Marcus, *The Age of Wire and String.*
Wallace Markfield, *Teitlebaum's Window.*
To an Early Grave.
David Markson, *Reader's Block.*
Wittgenstein's Mistress.
Carole Maso, *AVA.*
Ladislav Matejka and Krystyna Pomorska, eds., *Readings in Russian Poetics: Formalist and Structuralist Views.*
Harry Mathews, *Cigarettes.*
The Conversions.
The Human Country: New and Collected Stories.
The Journalist.
My Life in CIA.
Singular Pleasures.
The Sinking of the Odradek Stadium.
Tlooth.
Joseph McElroy, *Night Soul and Other Stories.*
Abdelwahab Meddeb, *Talismano.*
Gerhard Meier, *Isle of the Dead.*
Herman Melville, *The Confidence-Man.*
Amanda Michalopoulou, *I'd Like.*
Steven Millhauser, *The Barnum Museum.*
In the Penny Arcade.
Ralph J. Mills, Jr., *Essays on Poetry.*
Momus, *The Book of Jokes.*
Christine Montalbetti, *The Origin of Man.*
Western.
Olive Moore, *Spleen.*
Nicholas Mosley, *Accident.*
Assassins.
Catastrophe Practice.
Experience and Religion.
A Garden of Trees.
Hopeful Monsters.
Imago Bird.
Impossible Object.
Inventing God.
Judith.
Look at the Dark.
Natalie Natalia.
Serpent.
Time at War.
Warren Motte, *Fables of the Novel: French Fiction since 1990.*
Fiction Now: The French Novel in the 21st Century.
Oulipo: A Primer of Potential Literature.
Gerald Murnane, *Barley Patch.*
Inland.
Yves Navarre, *Our Share of Time.*
Sweet Tooth.
Dorothy Nelson, *In Night's City.*
Tar and Feathers.
Eshkol Nevo, *Homesick.*
Wilfrido D. Nolledo, *But for the Lovers.*
Flann O'Brien, *At Swim-Two-Birds.*
The Best of Myles.
The Dalkey Archive.
The Hard Life.
The Poor Mouth.

FOR A FULL LIST OF PUBLICATIONS, VISIT:
www.dalkeyarchive.com

SELECTED DALKEY ARCHIVE TITLES

The Third Policeman.
CLAUDE OLLIER, *The Mise-en-Scène.*
Wert and the Life Without End.
GIOVANNI ORELLI, *Walaschek's Dream.*
PATRIK OUŘEDNÍK, *Europeana.*
The Opportune Moment, 1855.
BORIS PAHOR, *Necropolis.*
FERNANDO DEL PASO, *News from the Empire.*
Palinuro of Mexico.
ROBERT PINGET, *The Inquisitory.*
Mahu or The Material.
Trio.
MANUEL PUIG, *Betrayed by Rita Hayworth.*
The Buenos Aires Affair.
Heartbreak Tango.
RAYMOND QUENEAU, *The Last Days.*
Odile.
Pierrot Mon Ami.
Saint Glinglin.
ANN QUIN, *Berg.*
Passages.
Three.
Tripticks.
ISHMAEL REED, *The Free-Lance Pallbearers.*
The Last Days of Louisiana Red.
Ishmael Reed: The Plays.
Juice!
Reckless Eyeballing.
The Terrible Threes.
The Terrible Twos.
Yellow Back Radio Broke-Down.
JASIA REICHARDT, *15 Journeys Warsaw to London.*
NOËLLE REVAZ, *With the Animals.*
JOÃO UBALDO RIBEIRO, *House of the Fortunate Buddhas.*
JEAN RICARDOU, *Place Names.*
RAINER MARIA RILKE, *The Notebooks of Malte Laurids Brigge.*
JULIÁN RÍOS, *The House of Ulysses.*
Larva: A Midsummer Night's Babel.
Poundemonium.
Procession of Shadows.
AUGUSTO ROA BASTOS, *I the Supreme.*
DANIËL ROBBERECHTS, *Arriving in Avignon.*
JEAN ROLIN, *The Explosion of the Radiator Hose.*
OLIVIER ROLIN, *Hotel Crystal.*
ALIX CLEO ROUBAUD, *Alix's Journal.*
JACQUES ROUBAUD, *The Form of a City Changes Faster, Alas, Than the Human Heart.*
The Great Fire of London.
Hortense in Exile.
Hortense Is Abducted.
The Loop.
Mathematics:
The Plurality of Worlds of Lewis.
The Princess Hoppy.
Some Thing Black.
RAYMOND ROUSSEL, *Impressions of Africa.*
VEDRANA RUDAN, *Night.*
STIG SÆTERBAKKEN, *Siamese.*
Self Control.
LYDIE SALVAYRE, *The Company of Ghosts.*
The Lecture.
The Power of Flies.
LUIS RAFAEL SÁNCHEZ, *Macho Camacho's Beat.*
SEVERO SARDUY, *Cobra & Maitreya.*
NATHALIE SARRAUTE, *Do You Hear Them?*
Martereau.
The Planetarium.
ARNO SCHMIDT, *Collected Novellas.*
Collected Stories.
Nobodaddy's Children.
Two Novels.
ASAF SCHURR, *Motti.*
GAIL SCOTT, *My Paris.*
DAMION SEARLS, *What We Were Doing and Where We Were Going.*
JUNE AKERS SEESE, *Is This What Other Women Feel Too?*
What Waiting Really Means.
BERNARD SHARE, *Inish.*
Transit.
VIKTOR SHKLOVSKY, *Bowstring.*
Knight's Move.
A Sentimental Journey: Memoirs 1917–1922.
Energy of Delusion: A Book on Plot.
Literature and Cinematography.
Theory of Prose.
Third Factory.
Zoo, or Letters Not about Love.
PIERRE SINIAC, *The Collaborators.*
KJERSTI A. SKOMSVOLD, *The Faster I Walk, the Smaller I Am.*
JOSEF ŠKVORECKÝ, *The Engineer of Human Souls.*
GILBERT SORRENTINO, *Aberration of Starlight.*
Blue Pastoral.
Crystal Vision.
Imaginative Qualities of Actual Things.
Mulligan Stew.
Pack of Lies.
Red the Fiend.
The Sky Changes.
Something Said.
Splendide-Hôtel.
Steelwork.
Under the Shadow.
W. M. SPACKMAN, *The Complete Fiction.*
ANDRZEJ STASIUK, *Dukla.*
Fado.
GERTRUDE STEIN, *The Making of Americans.*
A Novel of Thank You.
LARS SVENDSEN, *A Philosophy of Evil.*
PIOTR SZEWC, *Annihilation.*
GONÇALO M. TAVARES, *Jerusalem.*
Joseph Walser's Machine.
Learning to Pray in the Age of Technique.
LUCIAN DAN TEODOROVICI, *Our Circus Presents . . .*
NIKANOR TERATOLOGEN, *Assisted Living.*
STEFAN THEMERSON, *Hobson's Island.*
The Mystery of the Sardine.
Tom Harris.
TAEKO TOMIOKA, *Building Waves.*
JOHN TOOMEY, *Sleepwalker.*
JEAN-PHILIPPE TOUSSAINT, *The Bathroom.*
Camera.
Monsieur.
Reticence.
Running Away.
Self-Portrait Abroad.
Television.
The Truth about Marie.

SELECTED DALKEY ARCHIVE TITLES

Dumitru Tsepeneag, *Hotel Europa.*
The Necessary Marriage.
Pigeon Post.
Vain Art of the Fugue.
Esther Tusquets, *Stranded.*
Dubravka Ugresic, *Lend Me Your Character.*
Thank You for Not Reading.
Tor Ulven, *Replacement.*
Mati Unt, *Brecht at Night.*
Diary of a Blood Donor.
Things in the Night.
Álvaro Uribe and Olivia Sears, eds., *Best of Contemporary Mexican Fiction.*
Eloy Urroz, *Friction.*
The Obstacles.
Luisa Valenzuela, *Dark Desires and the Others.*
He Who Searches.
Paul Verhaeghen, *Omega Minor.*
Aglaja Veteranyi, *Why the Child Is Cooking in the Polenta.*
Boris Vian, *Heartsnatcher.*
Llorenç Villalonga, *The Dolls' Room.*
Toomas Vint, *An Unending Landscape.*
Ornela Vorpsi, *The Country Where No One Ever Dies.*
Austryn Wainhouse, *Hedyphagetica.*
Curtis White, *America's Magic Mountain.*
The Idea of Home.
Memories of My Father Watching TV.
Requiem.
Diane Williams, *Excitability: Selected Stories.*
Romancer Erector.
Douglas Woolf, *Wall to Wall.*
Ya! & John-Juan.
Jay Wright, *Polynomials and Pollen.*
The Presentable Art of Reading Absence.
Philip Wylie, *Generation of Vipers.*
Marguerite Young, *Angel in the Forest.*
Miss MacIntosh, My Darling.
Reyoung, *Unbabbling.*
Vlado Žabot, *The Succubus.*
Zoran Živković, *Hidden Camera.*
Louis Zukofsky, *Collected Fiction.*
Vitomil Zupan, *Minuet for Guitar.*
Scott Zwiren, *God Head.*